ANJALI JOSEPH was born in Bombay in 1978. She read English at Trinity College, Cambridge, and has taught English at the Sorbonne, written for the *Times of India* in Bombay and been a Commissioning Editor for *ELLE* (India). Her first novel, *Saraswati Park* (2010), won the Desmond Elliott Prize, the Betty Trask Prize and India's Vodafone Crossword Book Award for Fiction. *Another Country* is her second novel.

ALSO BY ANJALI JOSEPH

Saraswati Park

Another Country

❧

ANJALI JOSEPH

FOURTH ESTATE • *London*

Fourth Estate
An imprint of HarperCollins*Publishers*
1 London Bridge Street
London SE1 9GF

www.4thestate.co.uk

This Fourth Estate paperback edition published 2013

3

First published in Great Britain by Fourth Estate in 2012

A catalogue record for this book is
available from the British Library

ISBN 978-0-00-746279-7

Typeset in Minion by G&M Designs Limited,
Raunds, Northamptonshire
Printed and bound by CPI Group (UK) Ltd, Croydon, CR0 4YY

MIX
Paper from
responsible sources
FSC™ **FSC° C007454**

PARIS

1

Leela, self-conscious, released into the world, walked down the boulevard de Sébastopol. A September afternoon. Chestnut trees allowed their leaves to fall; the warm air carried them to the pavement. She had never seen leaves fall so slowly.

She'd been in Paris a week. She had found herself a studio apartment on the sixth floor of a building on the boulevard Saint-Denis, been to the offices of the language school, and obtained a copy of her contract. She'd gone to a branch of the Poste and tried to open a bank account. The woman behind the desk had looked at her sharply and said, 'Not only do you not have a Carte de Séjour, but you have a tourist visa. In ten days, Mademoiselle, you will be in situation irrégulière.' Leela realised this was the worst possible situation to be in. She burst into tears.

She went back to the Modern English School. The secretary, Mme Péron, looked upset. She said, 'But there is no problem. Go to the nearby branch of the Crédit Lyonnais. They know us.'

Leela opened an account. The next day, she took a train to London; Mme Péron had not applied for a work permit for her, forgetting that though Leela had lived a long time in England, she still had an Indian passport. A belated interview at the French Consulate had to take place.

In South Kensington her chest was x-rayed and she was examined by a French doctor. She was not tubercular, or illegal. She was granted a visa, and returned to Paris. When she had first arrived, a week earlier, it had been late summer, shadows long in the Tuileries. There had been ten days till Leela was to begin work, and she'd hoped to finish all the necessary tasks. Now, on her return, she was more realistic about the frustrations that awaited. It was suddenly autumn, the last autumn of the twentieth century: a cooler wind blew grit in the air, and on the boulevard de Sébastopol the leaves were falling in a very leisurely way indeed before they alighted on the street.

The simplest way to get to Patrick's house was to walk down the boulevard de Sébastopol till it hit the rue de Rivoli, then turn left. The rue de Rivoli became the rue Saint-Antoine, off which Patrick lived.

It was not the shortest route, but Leela was likely to become wildly lost even on a small mission near home. She had listened to Patrick's directions attentively, therefore, when she had spoken to him from London a few days earlier, but she now ignored them. She would go the way she knew.

In Haussmann Paris, the boulevards created vistas that implied grandeur. You were led past trees, impressive shops, and cast-iron-fenced square gardens in which elderly men sat on wooden benches looking, themselves, like overstuffed pieces of furniture. Later, there would be a focal point: a strange, neo-antique Egyptian column, or some Gothic remains. After that, more softly, the river and its joyous bridges. The sky opened out. But even as you wandered down the wide boulevards, examining the stone facades of buildings austere with established money, there was a feeling of being overseen and observed in a way Leela remembered from the largest court of her Cambridge college. Walking across this open space, in front of a neoclassical stone building, dwarfed by its scale and restricted to the paths that must be followed amid the sacred turf, she had not felt at home or welcomed, but breathed upon by pomp, and exposed in a large, cruel theatre.

There were other streets: the curving lanes of the Marais, through which she could have walked to reach Patrick's flat; or the alleys near the river on the Left Bank. But for one as constitutionally, as easily lost as she, it was necessary to stick to the boulevards and avenues. At least at first. On them, she loved the occasional diagonal cross street, as near the place Etienne Marcel: the slicing roads meant the last building before the open space was an etiolated triangle, as though a block had been turned into a slice of cake. They were rues transversales in French, a name that always felt magical to Leela, for these streets were not exposed to the eye in the same uncomfortably Olympian way as the boulevards; from them could arise surprises, chance meetings, the unexpected.

2

'Patrick, what are you *doing* here?' she asked.

His deep voice boomed out, good-natured. He liked to talk.

'Well, Leela, after college I did some temping. Mostly at an insurance company in Chelmsford. Taking a train every day to get there, then all day data entry, smoking breaks, the office canteen – they gave you a card and you charged it with money and used it to pay. Closed system.' He looked at her over his spectacles, raised bushy eyebrows.

'I'd get up early, at five, and read for an hour and a half before I had to leave so my brain didn't atrophy completely. The brain's a muscle, you know. That's what I keep telling my mother –' he turned to the side table and fiddled with the coffee pot, the sleeves of his white shirt flapping, ghostly. 'She doesn't use her brain enough so it's turning into the equivalent of my thighs.' He smiled, raised eyebrows at her again.

Leela was charmed. It made her bullish. 'But that sounds useful – at least you were reading,' she said. It bored her to be serious; however, her manner was almost always serious.

'No, you know, it wasn't, Leela,' he said. 'Because you just have two hours to insulate yourself against the world, and then you spend the whole day doing something completely asinine, repetitive – your brain could be turning to shit for all the world cares. That's why it's good you have a job like this, teaching, with time to yourself. The world doesn't care about your mind, after college. It's a shock in a way.'

They were getting off the subject. Leela was tense with trying to keep up. She felt an unspoken pressure to perform, and she performed badly under pressure. 'So why Paris?' she persisted.

'Well, I'm doing some consultancy work, technical writing, for two of the companies I worked for last year. And I'm writing a novel.'

'What's it about?'

'It's about a group of characters – it's difficult to explain. I think I'm stuck.'

'How much have you written?'

'Maybe thirty thousand words.'

'That's about half? A bit less?'

'Something like that. It's a big undertaking.'

'I'd love to read it,' she said. She felt hopelessly threatened. Writing a novel was a thing she'd dreamt of, and she was well past the age she'd set herself. She'd planned to be a prodigy, but had already turned twenty-one, an age when everything important seemed to be over.

'But why are you in Paris?' He smiled, and there was real sweetness in his face.

'I have this job, I told you,' Leela muttered.

'That's not what I'm asking.' She suspected he found her brusqueness half-charming; he knew that she liked him.

She glared.

Patrick grinned and rooted about the round table for his cigarettes. He found the packet, extracted one, looked at Leela, smiled to himself, located the matches, lit up, exhaled smoke and wellbeing. 'Why did you decide to come here?'

We're not really friends, she thought. I'm just some girl who likes him.

'I've always wanted to live in Paris,' she said. She thought of her first visit, walking early in the morning from the coach station towards the métro and the half-light, the cemetery, its rising wall, and Amy, enthusiastic in vest and shorts, carrying a huge rucksack, chattering unstoppably about friends at home as they passed things that Leela's heart had sung out were quintessentially Parisian – a cast-iron lamp post, or the tree next to it that sent a spray of leaves into the yellow light – until Leela had thought *I can't bear it any more* and said something, anything, to put an end to the stream.

Patrick said, 'Leela, I know we said we'd go out to eat, but I'm not really hungry I'm afraid – I got up late, I had a terrible hangover, and then I spent the afternoon tidying. It's the best way to deal with a sense of self-loathing. It's still messy in here –'.

'It's not messy,' she said. She looked around the flat, with its high ceiling and large windows. 'It reminds me of your room in college,' she said.

'It's nicer – but it's a little like that. Have some wine?'

'Thanks.' She accepted a glass, already dimly offended. He looked the same as in college, perhaps slightly more relaxed. His features, and the way he dressed, made him look older, but he wasn't old; he was a year older than she was.

The parts of his presence that she perceived – his height, his thinness, the mop of curly hair, his spectacles, a certain way of dressing, his wit, his oddness, his flashes of anger –

these would be her stamp of the ideal for some years to come. And yet they were accidental, weren't they?

'Let's go out,' he said a little later. 'A few of my friends are meeting round the corner, in an Irish pub. I'd like a drink, and you could meet them as well. They're nice.'

They left the flat, and she stood on the stairs while Patrick locked the door.

Stella was attractive, if not beautiful: she was slim and tall, and her brown hair was shiny and fell past her shoulders. Her mouth was painted. She was confident, and straightforward. She made Patrick laugh; Leela looked on, agonised. There was an older man, Craig, who owned an unspecified business; he was divorced, in his forties, his clothes and body comfortably untidy. He told Leela about his children, who lived in Amsterdam with their mother. Leela made conversation. She knew how: from an early age, she and her younger sister had been brought out at dinner parties to talk to the adults.

The pub was green-painted outside and in. There was a shamrock on its sign, and the whole group – Patrick, Stella, Craig, a blonde girl called Sarah who left early to meet her boyfriend, and another man, Simon – was delighted that unlike in most of Paris, here you could get beer by the pint. Leela reverted to a teenage habit and drank Guinness, slowly, to stop being hungry. By the second pint she was euphoric and nihilistic. The pub closed.

'We can go back to my flat, it's just round the corner,' Patrick said. He had wine, and a bottle of whisky. They sat at the long table, a convivial seminar group. Leela made fun of Patrick – she didn't know what else to do – and otherwise she was silent, taciturn when a question was asked of her, for she was bad at being in the spotlight. She worried about Stella.

'Oh, you teach at Modern? That's near my office, actually. Or not too far. We often go out round there. You should give me your number, let's go for a drink,' Stella said, and pleased though suspicious, Leela did, dictating it pretentiously in French. Stella's French was good. She was taking lessons. 'I'm going to be here for three years, so I thought, why not? It's not that I need it for work – most of our material comes in English – but it's an opportunity.'

She entered Leela's number in her mobile.

At two Craig, Simon, and Stella left. Patrick and Leela carried on chatting in the lamplight of the high-ceilinged room, its intensity and the fumes of whisky and cigarettes mimicking earlier meetings in earlier rooms. Patrick put on music.

'Is there something you'd like to hear?'

'Anything. Miles Davis.' Patrick had once told her he had learnt the trumpet for a while.

He was amused, and he put on a couple of tracks, then changed the music to something quiet and electronic. After a few minutes he smiled at Leela. 'Well,' she said, 'I think I'll go home.'

'All right.' He came to open the door. 'Are you sure you're going to be all right getting back?'

'I'll be fine,' she said. She would worry, she knew, about losing her way and being abroad in a strange city at a strange hour.

'Thanks for coming, Leela. Let me know if you're doing anything, and I'll let you know if I'm doing something,' Patrick said.

'Goodnight, thanks.'

She made her way down the narrow steps, across the courtyard and into the street. It was too late to take the overlit boulevards. She began to walk up the winding inside streets with their old town houses, trendy boutiques, small squares; in darkness and silence, avoiding anyone she saw. The street lamps shone and all was quiet, only the occasional cat running across the road, or a man who examined her face in the light but didn't comment. Near the school of the Arts et Métiers she felt better; she was in the third now, so it wasn't far. How tired she was, and how stupid to be walking alone. In the lamplight ahead was a lone figure on a bicycle. It seemed to be a girl with very short hair. The cyclist went slowly, almost meanderingly, just ahead of Leela, as though showing her the way. Yet when she slowed, Leela slowed too; they didn't meet, and the cyclist didn't force a confrontation. Near the rue Réaumur, near enough for even Leela no longer to be able to become lost, the cyclist turned in another direction. Only when Leela typed in the digicode, pushed the solid door of her bourgeois building, and heard it close behind her, did she begin to shiver with the awareness of danger undergone, and past.

3

Her bed was a narrow platform under the eaves of the Haussmann building. In it, she felt like the goblin visiting the student in Andersen's fairy tale. The beams were a foot from her head, and shed wood dust; for the first ten days she wheezed, and woke twice a night shouting, dreaming she was being buried alive. When she went to London for the visa interview, she bought four metres of white cotton in an Indian shop in Wembley. She swaddled the dark beams, and fixed the cloth with drawing pins. The dreams, and the coughing, stopped.

The flat was nineteen metres square, a figure she possessed with as much authority as her own measurements of height or weight. 'Studios are often twenty metres square. This one is small but it has everything,' said the landlord, M. Turgis. He was a psychiatrist, a good-looking auburn-haired man with bright blue eyes and a yellow smile; he lived on the fourth floor, where Leela went every month to pay the rent in cash. He would invite her in; the flat was elegantly furnished. For reasons she didn't understand, M. Turgis (not Dr, but M., he said) told her of his history. His mother was Norwegian. That explained the colouring of his two sons, pretty children of white-blond hair, fair skin, and the same bright blue eyes. The flat on the fourth floor had been in his family for some time; he had, he explained, bought three of the chambres de bonne on the sixth floor when they came up for sale in recent years. Now he rented them out. Leela was lucky, he said: the others had shared bathrooms, but hers was self-contained.

It was an odd shape; rather than being square, it was a parallelogram with a thin arm attached. In the parallelogram was the living room, with a bookshelf, a green plastic television set, a cheap blue carpet, a desk, a folding chair, and a floor cushion. A single, heavy window gave onto the narrow inner courtyard, and looked across at another such window. There was no view but sky, and the other window. Above the bookshelf, below the beams, was the blue-painted sleeping platform, reached by climbing a small wooden ladder. The platform was L-shaped; Leela slept near the ladder, snug against the external wall. On the other side was the slender corridor that ran down the sixth floor's maids' rooms. Here, lying in bed in the morning, masturbating serially, falling asleep midway then starting again, trying to work up the energy to begin the day – a period of time that, when she didn't have an early class, could persist until lunch – she heard the other inhabitants of the sixth floor hurrying out. Most were students; there was a Chinese man in his thirties, a foreign white man, where from she didn't know, and a young Chinese girl. M. Turgis' tread, more assured and heavier, theatrically careful, could also be heard from time to time, though she was relieved he didn't call on her often.

When she got up she would slide down the ladder, a move that became automatic, and go into the cramped white-tiled kitchen area, which held a small stove, a steel sink, a drop-leaf table, two chairs, a mop, and a blue and white kettle that she'd bought at the Monoprix on the boulevard. She would make coffee, and stare out of the window.

In the studio, everything needed for living had somehow been accommodated. Because it was well appointed, she tried to spend time in it as though it had been another space. On Sundays, she bought newspapers and croissants and sat on the living-room floor to eat breakfast and read. Quickly the size of the place would begin to weigh on her; rebelling against the obvious, she'd stay there. She'd turn on the television, or read one of the fat paperbacks she'd bought: *Les Misérables*, volumes 1 and 2; they were issued by different publishers so there was a gap between the two volumes, a lacuna that finally put paid to her desire to improve her French and follow the depressing fate of the convict Jean Valjean. She'd drink too much coffee, or overeat; she would use the telephone, and call her sister, who was usually out, or a friend; she'd imagine in great detail the things she would do later, and pore over listings in the *Pariscope*. She'd drink cheap wine, or smoke cigarettes she didn't enjoy, then worry for her health. It would begin to be dark outside, the sky fading through the heavy, viewless window, and the light of the window opposite coming on and brightening. It gave onto a room where often a man was standing, staring straight across, as though facing his fate. Leela would sometimes meet his eye when she stood at the sink, washing a cup; it dawned on her only after weeks that the facing room was the shared toilet, and that the man who occasionally turned to look into her face was holding his penis and urinating.

The apartment also held the memory of the time, in the early days of her occupation, when she had come down with a baffling fever and stomach ailment. For several days, all she

14

could do was lie on the foam mattress under the beams, and sweat and shiver, sleep and wake. She was hungry and had a headache but was unable to get down the ladder. She couldn't drink water, so didn't need to pee; that was a saving. The fever lasted for three days. Leela mused in between delirium on the indignity of such an end.

On the fourth day, when she managed to get down the ladder, her new, purplish-blue telephone began to beep, and its lights flash red and green. The voice on the other end of the line was warm: it was Nina, another of the new girls from work, saying she had had a terrible stomach bug. She'd had an idea Leela, too, might have been unwell. Could she come over, bringing aspirin, and something to drink?

4

Leela in a dark grey coat, dreaming on the escalator at St-Michel as it rose towards the air. An African man, bald, with a thick neck, had been staring at her on the train. He got off when she did. She'd looked back, uncertain, finally smiled to affirm she meant no harm, for he appeared irate. Suddenly a hand closed over hers on the rail. She jumped.

A deep voice behind her. 'You're African, aren't you?'

'What?' She pulled her hand away, moved up a step, turned to look. It was the man from the train, thickset and angry.

'You're African, aren't you, you little bitch?' He leant in closer.

'No.'

'You little snob. You're a half-caste.'

'Fu— Leave me alone,' she said. She darted away and climbed two steps at a time till the top. A slim birch tree burst out against the sky. She stood near the newspaper kiosk, shifty, waiting for the others. Six, hadn't they said six o'clock when they'd arranged to meet? They'd filed out of an interminable meeting for new and old teachers, and the three of them had gone to a café. She went into a telephone booth and dialled her answering machine. No message. Again she lurked, watching the passing European kids, and the French ones with their platform white sneakers, drainpipe jeans, and immensely long scarves.

'Sorry, sorry, sorry, sorry!'

Leela must first have looked annoyed, then laughed, for

Kate, slightly taller than she, was peering down, a Pierrot, thin, white-faced, with black brows pulled together in comical angst. When Nina, small, rosy-cheeked, blonde, arrived soon after, they discussed where to eat, then walked across the river back towards the Marais. Leela had seen a restaurant near St-Paul. On the way, Nina told them about her collocataire, Isabelle, and about the man she'd met at a concert a week earlier. 'I told my mother about it, eh, and she said, "I hope you remember you're not just representing yourself, you're representing your country."' She burst into laughter. 'I think she was telling me not to be a slapper.' Leela tried to imagine her own mother, thin, intense, saying, 'You're representing your country'.

Once across the river, they walked down an eighteenth-century street and into a pretty, almost twee square. There were restaurants on each side, spreading out awnings towards the trees next to cast-iron lamp posts. Strings of tiny bulbs gave the square a fairy-tale glimmer.

They were hungry, and sat outside under one of the tall, soldier-like heaters.

Nina asked, 'So where are you living, Kate?'

'I'm – it's really funny, I'm living with these two sisters, in the eighteenth, near the Batignolles?' Kate's inflection was upward, she widened her eyes and made clown-like faces of 'do you understand?' that Leela found endearing. 'I found it through this friend of mine. Her boyfriend knows these two girls, Amandine and Eloise. Their father left them on their own for a year, and they're dead young and they needed the money, so they've rented out a room.'

'Where's he gone?'

Kate wrinkled her nose. 'It's mental. He's gone on a sailing trip round the world with this woman he met or something. He gave the girls ten thousand francs and said have a good year. And Eloise is doing her licence, Amandine is doing her maîtrise. They're quite hippie-like though, it's cool. You should come and meet them. I think we're going to have a fête one of these days.' She laughed.

'What's your place like, Leela?'

Leela began to tell the story. Dusk had fallen, and it was colder. A sharp wind blew in the place, and the leaves bowled about, low flitting shadows. The air became blue and the light powdery.

Returning to the studio, she was amused, as though hearing again remarks they'd made through the evening. She felt the glow of laughter, of the wine, and the absurd, pretty lights in the vines around the bistro entrance. She wasn't, after all, alone. She opened the small door, let herself in, and turned on the lights, harsh against the night. The single window in the living area glinted; across the courtyard she saw the light had been left on in the corridor toilet. She was tired; instead of undressing and getting into bed, she moved about dreamily, taking out a book but not looking at it, playing a song to which she was at present attached. She thought of smoking, and didn't. Tiredness always took her this way, and the moment just after society found her as though congratulating or encouraging herself. See? Wasn't it all right? But this conversation gave way to a tiredness that became more profound, and a sense of the smallness, strangeness, and meanness of the studio, its cunning provisional arrangements, like the platform bed and the folding chair. She didn't go to bed for some time, for she didn't look forward to waking up in the silence of this strange cubbyhole, and it was the same silence, at first apparently interrogatory, but in no time again indifferent, unchanging, that met her now.

5

Rain: the day was chill and wore sad weeds. Inside the school, damp breathed through the corridors. Leela stood near the notice boards, unpacking her bag. Yes, her students' exercises were there, a file's worth of expensive paper, much of it squared and punched so that it could be filed; most people did their brief assignments on the 'copies' school children used. Pens, pencils, yes; hair band; tampons (she didn't take them out); wallet, keys (the heart always fluttered as the fingers probed in the satchel with faux nonchalance, then open desperation); random bits of paper and receipts; Carte Orange; the novel she was reading; unidentified fluff.

She began to put it back, in similar disorder. Now again, inevitably, it would take nearly a minute to locate the Carte Orange at the turnstile; finding her key at the hobbit-like door of the studio would lead to the usual cardiac suspension.

Towards the end of the repacking, a small hand patted her elbow. She heard Nina's friendly laugh. 'Did you lose something?'

'No, I just do this pathologically every time I arrive here or leave.' Leela scoped the corridor to see if any of her students were about; they were quite far away. 'I think it expresses my lack of composure about the job we do.'

Nina burst into an ongoing chuckle and held Leela's arm again. She was sharply dressed, her fair hair piled up, red lipstick matching her cherry-red boots; her stockings were lacy. She smiled at Leela's examination of her. 'You're developing the Parisian bitch-stare, eh.'

Leela laughed. 'I might be. I couldn't believe it when I first got here …'

Nina was still clutching her arm, and they began to walk towards the exit. 'I know, they're amazing, eh? That up-down when you get on the métro …'

'Yeah. "Those shoes with that dress?"'

Nina said, 'I went for a run the other day. I only took my Carte Orange and when I got on the métro at Tuileries these women were just looking at me because I was hot and sweaty and in a tracksuit.'

They were on the street, outside the school's seedy looking entrance. A man cycled by, grizzled hair close-cropped, charcoal clothes indefinably stylish. The rain mizzled down.

'What are you doing now?'

'I don't know,' said Leela, hesitant to suggest lunch.

'I've got loads of correcting to do.'

'Yeah, me too.'

'Want to come to my place? We could do our corrections together, maybe have something to eat? Nothing fancy, but I've got some nice cheese, and we could get some bread.'

'Okay, I'd love to.' Smiling, she let the other girl lead her towards the métro.

In the station their conversation became more muted, as though it were a misdemeanour to talk in English. They made their way to the platform, and sat on a bench. Both stared ahead, mesmerised by a pair of enormous posters. One showed a model in an embroidered top and jeans, smiling;

the second, the same model in the same pose, but wearing underwear that matched the outfit.

'Basically everything here is advertised with breasts?' Nina asked.

'Yep.'

'I saw a poster in a shoe shop in Les Halles, with a naked woman and a pair of sneakers.'

'Look at that.' Leela pointed at a furniture ad: a photograph of a sofa, over which a voluptuous yet toned naked woman sprawled.

'Hm.'

With a rushing and a clattering, the small train rattled into place, its lights flashing. Leela and Nina, an elderly lady near them, and a disaffected looking youth in baggy jeans and white hooded sweatshirt all moved towards the doors and reached for the handles.

The building Nina lived in was bourgeois in a quieter way than Leela's; smaller, more subdued. There was no elevator. They walked through a dark hall, up a wooden staircase and to the third floor. Doisneau, said the name plate. Nina brought out a key.

The flat was unexpected – why? It had all the traces of another life, an established life not like Leela's or her friends': a hall table, letters, bills, an umbrella stand, pictures; in the living room, two tall, shuttered windows that opened onto a balcony. There was a table in one corner, a divan bed, a kilim, and a succulent plant that looked insolently comfortable. Leela was surprised to feel a pang of longing.

'This is my room.'

She followed the other girl, who moved quickly, like a small nervous animal, pulling a curtain, opening a door.

The room was narrow and long; Nina's bed lay against a wall, and there was a desk, with her laptop, a plant, a bookshelf, a hanging wardrobe.

'It's lovely,' Leela said.

'Do you want to see my family?' Nina pointed at pictures in a collage on the wall: a balding, tall, outdoorsy man, and a plump woman with fine eyes stood outside a Scandinavian looking house on a hillside.

'I like your house,' Leela said.

'It's very typical of houses in New Zealand. There's a lot of modern architecture, and trying to bring the outside in. That's my brother.' This was a tall, blond young man, handsome but pained.

'He's gorgeous. Is he coming to visit?'

Nina laughed. 'No plans. He's a poet, did I tell you? Or he wants to be one.' She sighed. 'He's working in a petrol station, he's got no money. It's not easy.'

They passed again through the narrow room, into the small hallway, then back into the living room. Nina went to the kitchen, a neat, 1970s cupboard-lined area with colourful glass here and there, to make tea and take out the cheese. Her face crinkled. 'Do you feel like a little glass of wine? I have a bottle open.'

Leela laughed. 'Okay.'

They sat on either side of the table, their folders out and their faces growing warmer, their expressions more indistinct as they drank and laughed and ate cheese and bread and salad. A spear of sun slanted in through the window behind Nina, lighting part of her hair. Leela watched dust fall. She felt dazed, not by the wine, or the overtures of friendship as Nina told her more about Thomas, the guy from the concert. They'd gone out once or twice. 'It's not serious,' she said, but her face was eager. 'I'm not sure how much we have in common.' It was instead the unspoken sense of their homes, in other countries: Leela's a strange place familiar only from early childhood and emotion, the India to which her parents had unexpectedly returned, a place of silence, bird calls, a balcony next to her room, trees outside, and the life of the facing building; and Nina's, the modern house in an open landscape, near a beach where Christmas Day was celebrated with a barbeque, and a student world of working in a Mexican restaurant in Auckland, and not getting New Year's Eve off. For each girl, the other's home was non-concrete, but superstitiously to be believed, in the way of a story heard in infancy; it held a reality that had nothing to do with experience. Both knew it, and it made them feel tender, as though for their own lives, which might have been continuing elsewhere.

'I was wondering whether to bring him to Kate's party, eh?' Nina said.

'Party?'

'They're having a party on Friday, remember? Kate said we could bring people.'

Leela thought she would ring Patrick; she could legitimately invite him to a party, with real French people. Surely he'd be glad. She turned self-consciously to the page in front of her and looked for mistakes.

6

In the métro, Leela scrubbed surreptitiously at her cheeks. They flamed. It was possible she'd overdone the highlighting gel, which she'd found in the beauty department of the Monoprix while making last-minute preparations for the party.

She tried to catch her reflection in the window of the train; she was sitting on one of the fold-down seats near the door. Against the darkness of the tunnel, the glass was smeared with swiftly passing yellow lights and their comet-like tails. She glimpsed herself: hair up, brown skin, and large, comically anticipatory eyes. The person in the reflection was someone she recognised, but who it was hard to believe represented her. The cheeks, yes, they were sparkling away. She sat back. She would reassess, at Kate's.

In the last few years, she and Amy had made a ritual of getting ready. Wine, cheap and horrible, was procured; Amy blasted out her favourite music on the stereo; they would dissect the feelings and motivations of their friends and current love interests, long circling discussions that adduced, with all the precision of the legal mind, pieces of evidence and conversations and inferences from them, amounting, often, to an extenuating and essentially uncertain summation of psychological ontology: 'Maybe he's just insecure.' A phrase that became a joke between them.

Those moments of preparation contained aspiration, but also nervousness and self-obliteration – Amy, taking a palmful of foundation, would rub it all over her face, till her features were all but erased, then draw them back with eye- and lipliner, eyeshadow and mascara. In both girls, there had been a primitive uncertainty about cause and effect that still subsisted in Leela. It was what had led her to put a minimal dab of highlighter on her cheekbones then, unsure this would work, daub the stuff on her browbones, her temples, her collarbones, even her shoulders. The world was one thing, and it was colossal. One, next to it, was perpetually in danger of being forgotten. Tactics would have to be employed; but anxiety persisted about whether they would bear fruit.

'Have you seen our bathroom? Oh my God. You've got to see it. It's horrific.' On the last words, Kate's voice dropped to a stage whisper. She pushed the door.

Leela peered into a narrow chamber painted in black gloss. 'I love it!'

'Really?' The other girl looked disappointed. 'I think it's hanging, completely hanging. The girls' father did it.'

'Our dad is crazy,' Eloise said cheerfully to Leela. She and her elder sister liked Leela, who basked in their approval. Amandine was a sweet girl, reserved but warm, and would have been nice to anyone. But she nodded silently at her sister's summing up. 'Nina is sweet. But your French is better.'

Kate's room was unusual too: the walls were a deep, blue-red gloss that made it feel like a Chinese lac box. There was a single inadequate lamp, a sullen globe on the bedside table.

Leela put down her bag. 'Stay over,' Kate had said. 'You'd have to sleep in my bed, but it's big, don't worry.' The bed had an iron frame, slightly fairy-tale-like. Leela's mind drifted onto a sailing boat with Henri, the girls' wicked father who had abandoned them in order to bob on the ocean with his American sweetheart. 'It's an amazing flat,' she said.

'Isn't it?' said Kate dryly. 'Right, I've got to get ready. I'll just close the door. You don't mind if I strip off a bit, do you?'

She shut the doors into the passage and living room, and took off the floppy, flared black trousers she always wore, and a blue t-shirt. 'I feel so fat,' she muttered.

'You're not fat,' Leela said. She couldn't have judged the other girl's body as she would have her own: they were so different, Kate alabaster-white, straight-hipped, long-legged, but as she made embarrassed noises about herself and pulled on another pair of black trousers and a black shirt, and laughed, and said, 'Right', and opened the blinds again, Leela envied the differences.

The telephone in the hall started beeping; she heard Eloise's voice, saying 'Amandine!' and the other girl's murmur of protest from the kitchen where she was making tacos, then a flurry as the younger sister darted to the instrument. Leela had given Patrick the number in case he got lost; she had a premonition he'd arrived. She opened the door into the hall and saw Eloise, vigorous, certain, her blonde corkscrew curls bobbing. She was saying, 'Oui … oui … Ah!' and then in English, 'One minute. Leela!'

'I'm here,' Leela said.

'It's your friend – Patrick?'

Leela took the receiver. 'Hello?'

A few minutes later, the doorbell rang. It was Lucien, a childhood friend of the girls, and his girlfriend Claire. Just behind them, a familiar tall figure, booming as though to conceal embarrassment, 'Hello Leela. Bonjour, bonjour.' Eloise had come to the door and was smiling. Patrick bent to do his kisses, and Leela encountered the soft cheeks of Claire, a beautiful girl with short hair, and Lucien, a perhaps equally beautiful boy, short, dark-haired. Patrick and she, old acquaintances, didn't kiss; it would have been too weird. But he was clutching a bottle and they all came in, and no sooner were they in the living room than the bell rang again. Eloise rushed out, crying, 'Oh, it's starting!'

Leela, in one corner of the room, talked to Lucien and Claire about her job and their commuting. Claire was still living in Bordeaux, teaching and reading for the agrégation. 'I already have the CAPES,' she was explaining with a weary face. 'I just have to take the agrég, and then I can apply for a permanent job and we can live in the same place.' Lucien put his arm around her. The two of them were like appealing cartoon characters. Leela excused herself, and passed the chair where Patrick, still with his bottle of wine, now open at his feet, was sitting and accepting conversational overtures. Right now it was Eloise who crouched near him, lively and interested. 'What are you doing in Paris?' she was asking him in French.

Patrick's voice boomed out. 'Je suis flâneur. Je flâne.'

'You can't *say* that,' said Leela, scandalised.

'Non non, c'est bon, flâner, c'est ça,' said Eloise, thinking the disagreement was linguistic.

'Mais c'est tellement prétentieux,' objected Leela. She hated being corrected, and never knew why she felt the need to do it to others. She left them to the rest of the conversation and gave Patrick a disapproving look directed at the wine, which he'd informed her he had no intention of sharing since it was nicer than anything anyone else had brought. She went to the black bathroom, peed, and while washing her hands examined herself in the mirror, then scrubbed off the rest of the glitter. What had she been thinking? From the hall she heard voices, parts of conversation, and Amandine's laughter. Her boyfriend, tall and grave, was here now, and Eloise's boyfriend was expected. A bearded, red-haired boy, Thierry, was talking earnestly to Kate. Someone brought out a guitar.

'Salut,' Leela said. She smiled, and tilted her face for the inevitable kisses. Kate grinned at her. 'I can't wait to take out my lenses,' she said. 'Let's pretend to help clear up a bit.'

They carried sticky glasses into the kitchen. Amandine was doing the real cleaning. Eloise bustled, pleased with the evening; she dissected various strands of it. She passed them and smiled at Leela. 'He's nice, your friend,' she said. 'He's a bit spécial.'

Kate laughed, Leela too. 'Spécial, is that a good thing? Like special?'

'Mm. It's a bit like weird. But in a nice way,' Kate said.

'Oh yes. I see what you mean.'

'I like his nice deep voice,' Eloise said.

'He's funny, isn't he?' Leela couldn't decide whether she wanted to praise Patrick or for them to stop talking about him.

'Mm.'

'You girls can go to sleep if you want, I'm just going to tidy a bit, we'll do the rest tomorrow,' Amandine told Kate. She smiled at Leela, her pretty face patient.

'No, we'll help,' said Leela.

'Honestly,' said Kate in an undertone, 'there's no point, they'll be fannying about for a while, then they'll have their joint and go to sleep. Let's just crash. Aren't you tired?'

'Okay.'

The bed was large enough for them to face each other and talk in the half-darkness.

'Do they have a joint every night?'

Kate was nearly asleep. 'Yeah. Just a little one. They have it with their tisane or hot chocolate. Their mother grows the pot.'

'She's alive?'

Kate snorted. 'Yeah. But she lives in Provence. She's got a new family, a little son. Her husband's not that keen on the girls.'

'They couldn't live with her?'

'I think they're happier this way, to be honest. Though it's sad, isn't it …' Kate's voice dipped under the covers, a bird diving beneath waves.

'They're like little orphans,' Leela said. As so often, she was saddened by her interpretation of other people's loneliness.

'What did you think of Thierry?'

'He seems nice. He likes you, doesn't he?'

'He asked me out, but I'm not sure, I don't know.'

Leela was overwhelmed by the possibilities. 'You could see how you felt.' The darkness was closing in, their voices becoming distant from each other. Her own voice sounded unreal.

'Maybe … I dunno. Good night, our kid. Fais de bons rêves.'

'Good night,' said a sleepy voice, fading into the darkness.

7

Rushing up the stairs of the school, she bumped into the wall; she tried, as she climbed, to keep her still-damp hair out of her eyes, also to open her bag and examine its contents. Catastrophically, there wasn't time to take out and replace each item. She was late, and it wasn't even her class.

'*Oh!*'

She collided with something warm and felty. An arm came out towards her.

Leela, murderous but reflexively polite in this other language, muttered, 'Sorry! Sorry!'

'Ça va, mademoiselle?' The voice was deep, annoyingly mellifluous. She half looked up, as far as his chest, grabbed at her Carte Orange. It fell to the linoleum-covered step; she began to dive after it. The black-clad arm got there first. She noticed the hand: brownish, smooth-skinned, nails neatly shaped. She took a step back.

'Here.' The stranger held out the grey plastic case. Leela accepted it, forced herself to look at his face – all she wanted, ever, eternally, and in this specific moment, was to slide round the corner, hair over her face, all her possessions more or less attached to her. 'Thank you,' she said. The man smiled. He was in early middle age, dark-skinned, dark-haired, brooding, looked like he'd put his eyeliner on in a hurry.

'Excuse me,' Leela said. She smiled, skirted him, and continued to bolt up the stairs to the third floor. She scooted past the staff room; the door was ajar and she feared Mme

Sarraute, the coordinator of foreign teachers, would be standing there to watch her arrive late. As she reached room 3.14, she shoved the Carte Orange back into her bag, rooted around for the texts, and opened the door.

Four adults in their thirties and forties looked at her, tolerant but surprised. Leela began to explain herself, first in French, then, recalling the rules, in English. 'I know you're expecting Miss Molloy, but she's had to go to England for a few days. I'm taking her classes this week. I wonder if you'd mind introducing yourselves? My name's Leela Ghosh –' she pronounced it correctly, but they wouldn't '– and I also teach here –' pause for smile '– so, shall we begin?' She turned to the man, suited, crumpled looking, on the left of the semi-circle. The students, or clients as the school preferred to call them, sat on high chairs with a flip-out mini desk. The arrangement made them look like disgruntled toddlers.

'What's your name?' She produced an encouraging smile.

''Ello, I am Martin,' the man in the crumpled suit said. He smiled, first at Leela, then, a little more slyly, at the rest of the group. He pronounced his name as though it were English.

'Martin.' Leela smiled. 'And you?'

The stern looking woman next to him smiled. Leela saw an anxious high achiever. 'I am Catherine.'

'Hello Catherine. And –'

The door opened and the man from the stairs came in. He smiled silkily. 'Excuse me, I am late,' he said. He made his way to the empty seat near the door, took off his coat, and sat down with an air of contentment.

'Leela. Have another drink.' The whisky, golden and vaguely rank smelling, was already gurgling into her glass. 'It sounds like you need it.'

She smiled, and looked at Patrick, pouring the drink, and Simon, next to him.

'Totally,' Stella said. 'So he just followed you onto the bus? What a weirdo.'

'I didn't even realise, till he lurched towards me. I was trying to stamp my ticket, because my Carte Orange ran out this morning. I turned around, and he was leering at me and saying Mademoiselle. The bus braked, and I nearly fell over; he tried to steady me, but I pulled away, and I got off right then, when it stopped ...' She paused and looked around. She was aware of three people paying her attention: it made her stumble. She giggled. 'But he got off after me and stopped me in this really theatrical way, 'Mademoiselle, je vous prie!' and peered at me. You know, one of those people who bring their face really close to yours? He had a very deep voice and he said, "Did my gaze disturb you?"'

'Oh Jesus,' said Stella. Leela was aware of Patrick smiling at Stella, though he was still listening.

'Yeah, it was really cheesy.'

Simon chuckled. 'Then what did he do?'

'He said if I didn't go for coffee with him he'd feel terrible, and he had something very important to ask me, as one human being to another, and would I please just drink a cup of coffee with him for a quarter of an hour. And to be honest I didn't want to walk home and worry about him following me, because we were so close to my house by then, so I did.' She closed her eyes for a second. What she hadn't been able to recount, and felt queasy admitting even to herself, given the loathsomeness of Guillaume, for that was his name – was that when his hand had slid over hers in the bus, her first sensation, and perhaps the thing that had made her lurch, had been of its warmth and heterogeneity – the fact of being touched by someone else, who wanted to evoke something in her body. It had not been unpleasant. And yet, of course, she hadn't wanted it, a conflict that brought about inner revolt, and made her jump off the bus as it stopped.

'So what did he want?'

Leela sighed. 'I think he's just lonely. And weird. He wanted to talk about his wife, who's leaving him. He can't see his son and daughter, he's upset about that, naturally. He tried to persuade me to go for a drink with him.'

'I hope you didn't say yes?' Stella said.

'No, ugh, no. I told him it's against the rules of the school. He tried to argue and stuff but I said I had to go. I didn't want to walk towards my house, just in case. So I came back this way, and that's when –' Leela indicated Patrick '– I phoned. I hope I'm not intruding.'

'Leela, not at all. It sounds like a horrible day.' Patrick was as warm as ever, in as generalised a way; Stella too, in a way that both comforted and desolated Leela, for Stella sat close to Patrick and an unspoken complicity was between them. She was half aware also of Simon, watching her steadily and with some amusement. She looked at Patrick's hands on the table, square, reddish ('I have Irish farmer's hands,' he would declare) and at Simon's, curled around his glass. She couldn't read his expression; it was neither sympathetic nor indifferent, and this drew her to him.

'Leela, we were thinking of going out for a drink when you called. How does that sound?'

'Uh, yeah, sure.'

'We were thinking of going down the road to the Lizard Lounge.'

'Okay,' Leela said. She'd passed the bar, and marked it as too fashionable for her. But they walked down in pairs, Stella and Leela ahead, and Patrick and Simon behind, smoking. Leela was aware of Patrick talking and Simon laughing, then responding, and Patrick guffawing. She envied their ease. Stella was being sweet, though. She tucked her hair behind one ear and touched Leela's arm. 'I hope you're not feeling too weirded out by that creep,' she said. Leela wondered how much to play up the incident. Would it work? Would being wronged or vulnerable endear her to Patrick?

'It was a bit creepy,' she said. 'Especially because it happened near where I live. But I think it'll be all right.'

'That sort of thing keeps happening when you first move away,' Stella was saying as they neared the bar, from which dance music could be heard thumping. 'I remember when I was in South America –'

They were inside now, looking for a place to sit, and though the bar was dark and the music loud, the atmosphere was essentially civilised. The table was small, and cuboid leather stools were wedged around it. Stella threaded her way in, then Patrick. Leela sat next to Simon, their legs folded like jackknives, knees touching.

'What are you drinking?' he asked.

'I'm not sure. What are you drinking?'

'A beer.'

'Is it weird to have a kir after drinking whisky?'

He looked down at her, amused. 'Not if you want to.'

She asked the waitress for a vodka tonic. Simon and she sat watching her slender back as she walked away.

A song Leela knew came on. She began to hum along indistinctly. Simon grinned. She grinned back. 'Shit. Shouldn't sing in public. I may be slightly drunk.' He laughed, and patted her knee, a brief touch of a warm dry hand. The drinks arrived.

Simon was saying something, and she was distracted, smiling and leaning closer to hear, and also looking across the table where Patrick was partly hidden by Stella. He was laughing. Leela half closed her eyes to hear what Simon was saying. She glanced up to see Patrick looking at the two of them. He smiled at her, a smile so depressing that a hard resolve formed in her.

'There's something in your voice – a slight Irish accent,' she told Simon.

'Really?' He looked sceptical. 'I did live in Dublin for a couple of years, but that was a long time ago.'

'No, but the way you pronounce some words – something you just said, I can't place it but it was there. Dublin, how was that? I'd love to live there.'

'Have you been?'

'No … I've just read lots of books set there.'

'Joyce?'

'Joyce, and Beckett, and a couple of more recent things. This writer called Dermot Bolger.'

'*The Journey Home*? It's a great book.'

'It really is.' She was carried away with enthusiasm, a quiet part of her noting that the music had faded, and the bar seemed darker, or the lights travelling through space more blurry, slowing on their way to her. But if that's what he wants, she thought vindictively of Patrick, then decided to forget him. 'I've never met anyone else who's read it. Such a good book.'

'It is. And this other book I read when I was there – I suppose a sort of dumbed-down version of Joyce in a way,' he said. 'But I had a friend who read a lot and recommended it to me, very funny, *The Ginger Man*.'

'I loved it. That scene where he's trying to leave his wife and he's wearing her sweater …'

'And it's unravelling?'

'Yes.' She laughed. 'I read that when he was writing it he went to pubs and cafés with people and wrote down their stories and that's what he used for the book.'

Simon smiled at her. She smelled something, perhaps his scent – cologne, and under that, a fundamental smell of musk and perspiration, not unpleasant. An excited if uninvolved part of her noted it: You are smelling a new man. Another part, more sceptical, preserved a silence. Meanwhile, she was still talking. '… when I was younger, I mostly used to read American writers. Fitzgerald, Hemingway, Joseph Heller. A bit of Saul Bellow. I loved Salinger.'

'There's a perfect age to read all of that,' Simon was saying. She looked up at his face, skin a little tanned, lines around his eyes and mouth; he had delicate European skin that couldn't stand the sun. And his hair, sandy and thick, was tangled, a bit dry. His shirt looked unironed. But he was tall, broad-shouldered. She made these observations to herself, and a delight rose up in her: this was a reasonably handsome man, and he appeared to be interested in her. She coaxed herself: isn't this a good thing?

'So what were you doing in Dublin?' she was asking him, but the bar was closing. Or they were leaving. Definitely they were leaving. The bill appeared, and Simon, still talking to her, paid it. They were now outside, where the air was colder. Patrick lit a cigarette. He and his dark woollen jacket made a tall, familiar presence that caused Leela to ache.

Stella came up and patted Patrick's elbow. 'You'll walk me home, won't you?' she said.

'Of course.' He took a puff of his cigarette and smiled at Simon.

'I'll make sure Leela gets home,' Simon said.

How well they were arranging everything. Leela smiled, unsure whether to feel touched or irritated.

Stella came forward, smiling with genuine warmth. She kissed Leela on both cheeks, and said, 'Bye. It's been a horrible day, but it's over now. Just forget it.'

How does she know? Leela wondered, then remembered her earlier story. Oh yes. 'Thanks,' she managed.

Patrick patted her on the shoulder. 'Bye Leela. Call me, or I'll call you.'

'Sure.'

'Goodnight!'

'Goodnight!'

'Goodnight!'

Leela looked back. The figures of Patrick and Stella, seen from behind, were far away, self-contained as though in a painting. A fine drizzle began to fall, giving the air a lovely indeterminacy.

'Brr!'

Leela smiled. She pulled her thin jacket around her. They carried on walking, away from the others and into the pools of light under streetlamps. And now, nagged a voice inside her, now what will you do? She ignored it.

The pavement glittered with moisture.

Simon put a hand on her shoulder; she tried not to jump. He smiled. 'What were we talking about, anyway, before we were so rudely thrown out of that bar?' He released her shoulder, but not before his hand had been there long enough to signal deliberateness. It was a charming gesture, and made her nervous. She took refuge in seriousness.

'I guess the waiting staff wanted to go home ...'

He shrugged. 'Oh well. It's not like we didn't leave in time.'

'No.'

They walked on. She made an effort. 'You were telling me about when you lived in Dublin. What were you doing when you were there?'

He smiled. 'Work, for the company before this one. I do some consultancy, you know. It's business development essentially. Boring, boring –' He waved it away. Leela was still examining him; it struck her there was something grave, disciplined about him, perhaps also something adamantine. She scolded herself: there was no need to narrate the experience before it happened. Her feet, in sandals, were cold; she stumbled. Simon put out a hand and caught her elbow. The hand rubbed her back between the shoulder blades, rested on one shoulder. He was good at doing this, she noted – touching in an exploratory fashion that managed to seem merely friendly. Perhaps, argued her brain, it *is* merely friendly. 'Dublin,' he said. The hand cupped her scapula and smoothed it out, let it go, rested warm and innocuous on the muscles aside it. 'It's a great city, we had some really good times there.'

'Where else have you lived?'

The hand smoothed the side of her upper arm.

'Lisbon for a bit – a long time ago. South America for a while.'

'Where?'

'Rio … Here.' They turned up the rue Vieille du Temple. It was late, a weekday evening, and the bars and cafés whose life bloomed onto the narrow street in the day were shut now, pulled into themselves. The pavements were clear, only lamplight shattering on damp macadam. She followed its Deco starbursts. They passed the café called Les Philosophes, and another place she and Nina had once gone, an odd little bar with sun lamps, where Belgian white beer was served in litre tankards.

'You're quiet,' Simon said. 'Here, we should take another right. I'll show you where I live, then you can drop in if you're passing.'

Up a silent street, where old buildings leaned into the darkened road. They passed massive doors. Simon paused outside one. A traffic sign, a white circle ringed in red, said ACCÈS with a red diagonal crossing it.

Simon wasn't holding her arm any more. He stood in the street, not far away, his face more than half in shadow, and his voice slightly nervous. 'Come in for a drink?' he said. 'See the flat?'

She hesitated, but the next day was a respite without classes; she always timed a weekly adventure or crisis for this night, and slept half the free day away, as though from nerves, or loneliness. 'Sure,' she said.

He grinned, she thought, in the dark, and turned to put in the digicode. The lock clicked, and he pushed one of the great doors. Leela stepped over the threshold.

The stone stairway was cold and damp; the flat was on the second floor, with a burgundy door. Simon used his key, and Leela went in. A dark crowded hallway – a small wooden table, boots near a closet with a half-open door, and, 'Here,' said Simon, 'come into the main room.'

It was very large, with two big sofas, and a white wall of shelving, in which were neatly arranged paperbacks, and various other objects: cigarettes, a road map of the Île-de-France, a glass ashtray, a box of mints, black and grey plastic film canisters, keys, coins, and a scuffed copy of *In Cold Blood*, splayed open on its front. The room reminded Leela of a larger, airier version of an Oxbridge fellow's study, and she felt impersonally indulged, welcomed in the way students always were in those rooms – seated on a sofa and given coffee or a drink to sip.

'Beautiful room,' she said. She looked up at the high ceiling.

'Isn't it great?' Simon's hand rested briefly on her shoulder. He walked past, to the coffee table, and removed a mug, piled up a few large books, flicked at a cushion. 'This room is really why I took the flat. Well, that and the upstairs. Come with me, I'm going to the kitchen to get us a drink.'

He walked out, and Leela followed him, into the hallway and then a small, plant-filled kitchen. 'The lady whose house it is asked if I'd be willing to look after the plants,' he said, smiling at Leela. She brushed gingerly past a large spider plant, whose leggy babies, each on a long stalk, were reaching for the floor tiles.

Simon was opening a cupboard. 'Would you like a drink-drink? A gin and tonic, or a vodka?'

Leela hesitated. He grinned, his hand on the cupboard door. 'You can have anything you like. Even if it's non-alcoholic.'

'Do you – can I have some tea?'

'Tea?' His grin was wide, but not without warmth. 'Sure you can. With milk and sugar? Real tea?'

She nodded. He smiled to himself as he filled up the kettle. 'A cup of tea.' While it was boiling, he got out tea bags – Assam, she noted sadly – a jar of sugar, and a tall glass. She watched him move around the kitchen, and, looking at the red mela-mine counter, scored in places, she felt a fleeting affection for the family life that might have gone on here earlier.

Simon worked methodically, unhurried: he took tonic out of the fridge, and a lime, sliced it, got the ice cubes and so on as he made his drink. Leela watched. She was aware that he didn't really care whether or not she had been there, and this made her relax and warm to him in a way she would have found difficult to explain.

He took out the tea bag, smiled at her, put in milk, and – which also made her warm to him – two and a half spoons of sugar without comment, stirred it, gave her the mug. He picked up his own glass.

'Let's go through to the other room.'

Leela followed him, and he put on a floor lamp near the back sofa and sat down. The room was dim, hospitable. The enormous windows gave onto a damp, dark blue night.

Leela sat on the same sofa, and sipped her tea. It was too hot. She put it down.

'Just a second.' Simon got up and went towards the kitchen. He was gone for a little while, and she reached for the heavy art book in front of her, a collection of photographs entitled *Doorways*. She leafed through it randomly: entrances in what looked like Mexico, some that seemed to be here in Paris, London, she thought …

Simon returned, smoking, carrying another ashtray. He stood looking down at her. 'Like the book?'

She smiled at him. 'It's interesting. Lots of, well, doorways.'

He laughed, and ruffled his hair. It made him look older, and slightly wild. 'Yeah, it's always good to have an eye at the exit, isn't it?' He put the cigarette in the ashtray, put the ashtray down, eyed Leela with a quick calculating glance that the quiet part of her consciousness noted – but wait and see

45

what happens, urged the rest of her mind – sat down, leaned quickly over and kissed her. He took one shoulder to keep her steady, and she cooperatively kissed him back, noticing that his lips were soft, that he pushed his tongue into her mouth too soon but withdrew it as quickly, that he was good at this, that it wasn't having any effect on her beyond the most automatic physical arousal, and that he tasted of both cigarettes and mint.

He pulled back, smiled at her, a smile of elation with himself. 'Stay here tonight?'

Leela, the eternal wanderer with no destination to aim for, said, 'Okay.'

'Come and see the bedroom.' He jumped up, pulled her with him, raised his eyebrows, mocking the moment. She laughed. He came back for his drink. The cigarette had gone out. Leela followed him, turning at the door to look at her abandoned mug of tea.

The staircase was narrow, the carpet plush and thick; she followed Simon up it, looking at his bum and wondering with the usual self-amusement if she was really about to become better acquainted with it. His trousers looked vaguely dad-like, she worried. Atop the stairs was an opening. She stepped into a large attic, with two skylights and pale blue walls. The bed was a white, messy island.

'It's a lovely room,' she said, but Simon was bending to kiss her again, more intent, and his expression – she kept her eyes open, alarmed at herself – was completely serious, admitting of no humour. She felt self-conscious, she wanted to make a joke; she put up her arms to hold his upper arms, and he put a hand up her top, moved aside her bra to rub her nipple, a gesture that made her flinch, or shiver, she wasn't sure.

When she woke it was early. Cold morning came through the skylights. Simon slept on his back, his breathing audible, like a standing fan. One arm came out of the covers. His hair was rumpled. She felt no desire to touch him, and recollected their long and exhausting feints in bed – the various things he'd done, with which she'd cooperated, increasingly wishing she'd gone home: his putting his fingers roughly into her to feel her wetness, then licking her, something she found intensely embarrassing, and this time, not particularly arousing, and finally sex. She had thought she might come, but hadn't; had wondered whether to pretend, however that was done, but hadn't; he had persisted for a long time before finishing. After that he'd tried to touch her, instructing her to move against his hand, but she'd said instead that she was tired, and he had rolled over. How was it possible, when you'd had an apparently urbane, socially competent time earlier, to find yourselves behaving so ineptly when unclothed? She had failed, she supposed; yet, obstinately, she still wanted to be loved.

Confused, parched, and with an incipient headache, she got up from the edge of the bed where she'd lain all night for fear of being caressed in sleep, or the desire that if this happened it should be done deliberately. There were her clothes, strewn about the floor. She picked them up, looked back at Simon, who snuffled and moved the arm that hung off the bed. There was a book on the floor. She moved it to the armchair, then tiptoed down the stairs with her clothes clutched to her. In the beautiful living room, hunched near the bookshelves where she was least visible from the street, she put on her clothes, first her bra, then her pants, wincing at the slight soreness. She looked round the room when dressed, as though to gauge its expression – would she and this place meet again? In the bleached light, the furniture was impassive.

Near the hall table, next to Simon's desert boots, she found her shoes and pulled them on. She managed to slide back the door bolt, and shut the door behind her. The landing and stairwell were now those of many Parisian buildings. As she walked through the cold interior courtyard, the stone was slimy with dew; black plastic bags gave off overripe odours.

She briefly feared the outer door wouldn't let her leave, but she found the button to press and slipped into the street. It was raining, and cold. She walked slowly home, reassured by the quotidian misery of the Monoprix, with its fluorescent lights on against the dim day. It was eight o'clock. She bought bread, milk, and coffee. As she crossed the road towards her building, she saw in the alcove of the Crédit Lyonnais the mad old woman, wrapped in her layers of clothing, sitting on the stone ledge. She held a Styrofoam cup of coffee in claw-like fingers. Leela walked towards her, trying not to look, and angry eyes burned into hers. The old woman spat.

In the studio, Leela took a shower, then made coffee. She turned on the television, the lights, the electric heater, and sat on the floor cushion. Late episodes of *The Bold and the Beautiful*, dubbed into French, were airing, and she watched one, depressed by the huge jaws of the men, their suits, the women's heels and tans and bouffant hair. The rain became louder, smashing on the thick pane of the single window. Leela imagined floods, people's cold, wet stockinged feet on the tarmac outside, bus horns, Paris cursing. She didn't have to go to work. She thought of Simon, when they'd been chatting in the kitchen, saying he kept his car in a garage nearby, that they should take it out and go for a drive in the country one weekend, and she wondered abstractly and yet inquisitively, as a child to whom something has been promised, whether this would happen. Maybe Simon would be her boyfriend? She imagined them doing the things couples did – being seen here and there – and she pictured Patrick's face when he saw them. But she could see it as nothing other than pleased, if surprised, and she stopped thinking of it and hunched tighter on the floor cushion.

When the programme ended, she went to wash the cup and cafetière, and saw the Chinese student in the window opposite. The air outside was dark and stormy; the light in the toilet was on, and while she washed up she glanced across and thought how cold the little cubicle must be. When the man in the facing window made a gesture of privacy – buttoning up his trousers – he lifted his head and turned, as though drawn to the facing light in her window, and she thought their eyes met for a moment before, embarrassed, even slightly sad, both quickly turned away.

8

'Who's there?'

Leela froze, her hand still out, and wondered if she'd forgotten herself sufficiently to have replaced 'hello' with 'knock knock'.

'Um, sorry?' she said.

He laughed. He was dark-haired, slightly lantern-jawed, handsome in the alienating way of Captain America.

'Just joking. I meant, who're you? I'm Greg.' He was definitely not French; she thought she heard the Home Counties in his accent.

'Oh, hi Greg.' She felt relieved, as well as shifty, clutching her plastic cup of red wine. She'd helped lug the bottles up when classes ended that afternoon. Attendance at the monthly school social – an opportunity for students to practise their English with teachers in an informal setting – was obligatory. 'I'm Leela.'

The fluorescent lights were bright, it was seven forty-five, and three of her students were across the room, looking around, diffident but hopeful, avoiding the wine.

'Hi Leela.' He smiled at her. The corners of his eyes crinkled. Something about him made her feel despair.

Across the room she saw Guillaume, ratty and smooth in his good coat. He was talking intently to a young woman who seemed to want to get away. When Leela's eyes met his, he ignored her.

She wasn't sure Greg wanted to talk to her, but he had begun the conversation. She ought to be offering herself up to yet another dialogue with a stammering, forceful student. But she'd done that for nearly two hours.

'Do you work here?' Across the room, she saw with envy that Nina and another teacher, an Irish girl called Tessa, were laughing together, again in contravention of the rules, and pouring each other wine.

'No, I'm living with one of the tutors, I mean I'm sharing his flat.'

'Oh, who's that?' Leela was having a hard time focusing on his face. Why? It was a well-appointed face. His dark hair, pushed back, made a curl then flopped like a waterfall over his brow.

There's nothing behind his face, she thought, and realised he had been speaking.

'Where do you live?' He said it patiently, as though speaking through glue, probably for the second time. Must concentrate.

'Oh, on the boulevard Saint-Denis.'

'Ha ha, really?'

'The *boulevard* Saint-Denis,' Leela repeated. 'Not the rue Saint-Denis. It's perpendicular. At the north end of the rue Saint-Denis.'

'But it's quite something, isn't it, that street? God!'

His face became earnest, his eyebrows wavered; she noticed his black jacket, well cut, and the thin cotton scarf wrapped several times around his throat, mentally clocked the time and energy he must have put into assembling this look. Again she had the strange, unwelcome sense that behind it all, scarf, handsomeness, jacket, there was nothing: shadows in the sunshine day.

'How do you mean?'

'Well, all those ads in phone booths, those little doorways – video parlours.' His eyes bulged at her, and she suspected him. 'It's pretty depressing, isn't it?'

Leela thought of Baudelaire's consumptive girlfriend; she was still there, but today she lived up a narrow staircase, and had to fuck businessmen and be videoed while she did it, a piece of paper with 'virgin, just arrived' written on it in the doorway below.

She had an intense urge to get away from Greg.

'I've got to – excuse me.' She smiled and walked towards Nina and Tessa, who were laughing and drinking across the room in his line of sight.

'Hm, he's lovely, who's that?' Tessa enquired.

'Some guy, he's living with Jim Davis.'

'He's cute,' Nina said. 'Listen, my brother's coming here for a visit in a few days. Are you free on Sunday? We were maybe going to go out for lunch.'

'That sounds great,' Leela said.

Nina lowered her voice. 'Hey, what's happening with that man you met?'

'Simon? I don't know. I haven't heard from him in a bit.'

Before the end of the evening, Leela, now much drunker, sought out Greg again. His eyes flashed alarm when she approached, but she talked to him for ten minutes, discovered that they had grown up not far away from each other – though he must have had a genteel, quite English set of parents, and, she thought, a minor public school education – and discussed with him his interest in amateur theatre. Like her, he felt he didn't see enough plays. There was Shakespeare in the twentieth somewhere that week. She gave him her telephone number.

'I'll call you,' he said, his eyes frightened.

She went home inebriated and truculent, and stayed up too late.

In the morning, the day was clear and mild, and the flat was filling with water. Her green television bobbed on clean water; sun spilled into the room and refracted from small waves; water rose towards her platform bed. She sat up, slid down the ladder, and dipped in a toe. It was warm. She sighed, slid in, swam to the kitchen, out of the front door, down the corridor, and out of a window. Paris was submerged. The sun shone. She swam towards the top of the Tour Saint Jacques. Prostitutes from the rue Saint-Denis swam past, and a bus driver. She knew she was dreaming, but felt she was about to find out something important; she tried to stay in the dream even as she woke. Rain was beating on the heavy glass window; her fingers were chilled and slow.

That night, she couldn't sleep. Disoriented, she walked to the kitchen, got water, turned down the blast of the heater, wondered, and silently enquired of her surroundings, like the white-glaring kitchen tiles, What do you want from me?

She turned on the television: nothing; turned it off, sat exhausted on the floor cushion. The space was snug around her, a small cabin in a large ship.

She got up and put on a cassette, the first of two in a neat cover printed: 'Le Nouvel Italien sans peine'.

Paolo was telephoning Marco.

Marco non è a casa.

'Marco non è a casa,' repeated Leela joyously, freed from embarrassment. It was three in the morning; the world was closed for business.

'Who's calling?' the woman who had answered asked.

Sono Paolo.

Ciao Paolo. Sono Francesca.

'Ciao Francesca!' Leela repeated with Paolo.

Marco was not at home, but Francesca would tell him that Paolo had called. He would be back later; he had gone out. How long was Paolo in Milan?

Leela rewound the dialogue. Though she had moved on to other lessons, she remained attached to the simplicity, perhaps the stupidity of this one, which constituted its sweetness. How transparent they were, Francesca and Paolo! Francesca in a householderly way withheld her identity until she'd verified Paolo's. The two of them shared their Dantesque names without chuckling over the fact; and Marco, ineffable, slightly mysterious, yet obviously lovable and loved, Marco was not at home.

She spent the next five minutes replaying in her head the conversation she, after a pause of hesitation, had had with Simon's answering machine two days earlier. At the start of the week, he had telephoned, said that 'the other night' had been fun, asked what she was doing at the weekend, and said he had to go to Dijon for work but would be back on Friday. 'Maybe we can do something?'

Why had his apparent diffidence not rung true?

'Yeah, sure, I'm around,' she'd said quickly.

'Great, give me a call.'

She'd called on Friday afternoon and left a message; it was now Saturday night, and she hadn't heard from him. Perhaps he'd stayed in Dijon for the weekend? Perhaps he had friends there? Perhaps he'd met someone, or he wasn't interested. But he'd said – he'd asked her. But his tone of voice –

She didn't want to think about this, and would think about it for hours tonight while time failed to unspool under the fluorescent light. She searched for a cigarette and found one with a baggy fold. She lit it at the cooker and began to smoke without pleasure. The tape whirred and clicked. She pressed play.

'Premier dialogue. Un appel de téléphone.'
Pronto.
Buongiorno. E possibile di parlare con Marco, per favore?
Marco non è a casa.

The next day at twelve thirty she came out of the métro at Saint-Paul. The carrousel was still and the day cold, the light sharp. Nina arrived, rosy and pleased, with a tall blond young man who smiled. He said hi to Leela and performed the cheek-kissing with her and Kate, who arrived a minute later. They went to the café nearby that Nina liked.

Leela enquired about the quiche of the day.

The waiter looked down at her hand. 'Don't forget to buy your ticket, Mademoiselle,' he said.

Leela glanced down at the writing on her left hand and grinned. 'I have to buy a train ticket. I'm going home to London for Christmas.'

The world of the café opened out; indistinct but loud, she heard the conversations of others, and felt the daylight filtering through and reflecting from the large plate glass windows. Nina's brother smiled at her.

9

He carried on moving his mouth in sleep, Simon, as though saying unknown words to absent people. It amused Leela, and alarmed her, a moment of what might almost have been intimacy. She'd woken a few minutes earlier, beginning to be conscious that sleep was still near. From the skylight the grey morning flooded in. She sidestepped the accumulation of encouraging things she'd said to herself last night about Simon, about Simon and herself. In the first instant of waking, her mind sharpened itself, and began by distinguishing itself from everything else: the pale light, the bed sheets, the body next to her. The self examined itself and found no rancour: simply, it noted, this wasn't it.

Leela squirmed. 'Why not? Why not this?' she pursued.

Silence.

She put an arm under her head, slid a little away from Simon, and examined him. The skin around his eyes frightened her in the mornings; it looked so old and belaboured. When they were both awake, cooking, drinking, talking, even in bed, the presumption of parity in their ages held; she was never certain enough of herself to know how they related to each other. Now, though, she was appalled by what time could do: how it gathered and stayed in the skin.

Simon woke and sighed. He lay gazing at the skylight then suddenly put a hand on the far side of Leela's waist and rolled her over. He looked into her eyes, closed his, sighed, kissed her, felt her bottom.

'Morning,' she said self-consciously.

'Morning,' he said at length, the dry politeness of his voice a considerable interval from what his hands and body were doing.

'Right,' he said, swinging up and out of bed. He began to dress at once. Now she saw him wearing jeans, a white t-shirt, a flannel shirt on top. He frowned, sitting on the bed to put on socks, his shoulders tense. The abruptness with which he peeled himself away from her, and the way her skin, which had been warm against his, was left exposed to the cold air, disconcerted her.

'I'm gonna make some coffee,' he murmured, and began to disappear down the stairs.

Leela, alone under the skylight, picked up her clothes then went to the bathroom to shower – the water was never quite hot or plentiful enough – and dress. She examined her face in the mirrored bathroom cabinet and was surprised by its youth, how unmarked it was. Her hair sat flat. She fiddled with it and gave up.

In the kitchen, she found Simon plunging the top of the cafetière. Seen from behind, he in every way signified a man: his height, the dishevelled hair, his wide shoulders and the swoop of his back and shirt into his jeans.

She came to rest at his side, and he handed her a cup of coffee. She followed him to the living room, and remembered with a movement of shame, but also amusement, her relief of the evening earlier this week when he'd phoned, his voice both lazy and nervous, to ask if she were free. Leela, clutching the blue receiver, had been abruptly lightened: the world had become less cruel.

She carried an immoderately-sized bag and struggled through the Gare du Nord, away from the suburban trains and the orange 1970s decor and with relief onto a sleek glass-sided escalator, towards the Eurostar. A ticket slid into a machine at the turnstile, a space-age version of the métro. She queued along airport-like corridors and passed shining pillars, walked down a smooth cream slope into the train.

She heaved the holdall into a luggage rack and slid into a seat at the window. Its partner remained empty for a long time, and she adjusted her consciousness with pleasure to the unexpected space. Just before the train left an attractive young black woman appeared, toting a toddler and various bags. She accepted aid from a male passenger to stow her things, and sat down next to Leela, sighing. The train moved out of the station, through wrought-iron arches. Then they were in open country.

But the baby soon shat itself, and the mother, despite having smiled at Leela and returned her greeting when she sat, despite being young and well-dressed and attractive, if a little harried, merely sat there for two and a half hours, not changing his nappy. Leela considered moving, or going to the dining car – something, anything. The infant squirmed, and periodically cried, but he and certainly his mother appeared to bear it all stoically. Leela, uninvolved in their arrangement, resented having to do the same. It smelt. You smell, she thought, regarding the pretty little boy with some distress. He cried and held out his hands to her, I'm sitting in my own shit, help me. No, no, she thought. His mother shrugged and laughed, charming but implacable. Leela tried to read her magazine.

Patrick McCarthy was on a train too, but he was already in England. He opened a letter from his sister, already read, and reread a particular paragraph. The train shook its way through East Anglia. He leant back, breathing in air that was stale from the heaters, and sharp when it mixed with cold air from the windows. Fields in winter, the stubble razed and the ground hard, unrolled in a fine golden light.

After all, he felt affection, a stirring in his self, for this soil and this country. He denied it when he was away, even as far as London, but something in him was content to be at his parents' and do simple things: walk to the pub for Christmas Eve drinks, get in the car and drive to the supermarket, or have a pointless argument with Camille, wind her up over nothing. It was getting harder to do that: she stopped herself even as her cheeks began to redden, and laughed at him.

Hampstead, the attic room last night. He'd slept just next to the bookshelf, which made a partition in the room; the eyes of that girl, blue but bordered with something darker, and her loose red mouth as she talked, the way it appeared to move wildly, unrelated to the words he heard in her voice, Simon's arm and his white torso, the conversation yesterday when they started on the whisky, his feeling of warmth, the creakiness of the floorboards on which his mattress rested, the quiet in the morning, his headache, the light and bustle at the station, a peculiar smell of winter, even of Christmas, again Simon and one of the jokes from last night; he'd forgotten the punchline but he remembered their laughter and someone else's face, Simon's mouth, that girl's eyes, smoke around the table, his own warmth inside (the whisky) and cold in general (the flat), the sense of London spread out around them in the dark, a darkness into which their own names, particularity, importance at this social occasion, their place, in short, completely disappeared: all these and other impressions lay jumbled untidy like dirty cards from a pack that he would have to keep seeing until he could put them in some sort of order. For he'd been drunk, and tired, and so although he had been there, gathering these images, apparently he had also been absent. Where had he been then, while the images were impressing themselves in a store, now to reappear and shuffle randomly until they could be viewed, classified, and put away? It was this he liked least in a hangover.

The train stopped at Manningtree, then started again: a dirty, wide estuary opened under the sky.

No one was home. Fresh from the exertions of lugging her bag through the underground, Leela knocked on different parts of the door, tried the bell. She put down the bag, walked round the house, on a street stacked with other such houses, under a plain east London sky, all air and greyness. She sat on the bag. An elderly man in a long collarless coat passed, seemingly raising an eyebrow; his white geometric beard turned away from her. She saw the hem of his kurta emerge from his coat, and felt embarrassed. Another pair of younger, bearded men. Leela looked away.

'Ah!' Amy's cry was all of pleasure; it was nonetheless formidable. Leela allowed herself to be swept into a hug, then led to the door.

'Oh no, oh no,' Amy murmured as she attacked the door and rummaged in her bag. 'Aaah. Thought I'd lost the keys again.'

They went in, Leela behind her friend, a flurry of voice and red hair, and then the house, surprisingly modern: steel and leather furniture, expensive sofas.

'It's very plush,' Leela said.

'Uh, well, I think it's a bit fucking expensive. I'd rather live somewhere grottier and cheaper, but the boys found it.'

'Well, at least it's nice.'

'Let's get a cup of tea. I told them I was sick at work, to get out in time for you, and now I think I actually am feeling sick.'

'Oh no!'

'Boring, boring,' agreed Amy viciously, whacking tea bags into not very clean mugs. 'It's disgusting here, disgusting. No one's washed up in weeks. We're paying a cleaner a hundred quid to come round and sort it out. I'd do it myself for that much money but I can't suggest that.'

They took their mugs up the stairs, into a room that was warm and furnished with all the items Leela recognised as characteristic of her friend: a thick duvet, crumpled into a strange shape; clothes on the floor; black shoes of two types, either high-heeled and intimidating, or flat and mannish, all scuffed and tossed on the ground.

Amy stooped, dived into a pile of laundry, emerged with something frilled and pink and used it to tie up her hair: a pair of knickers. 'They're clean,' she said.

Leela grinned. 'I've got a present for you in my bag.'

'Oh, lovely! I don't have your Christmas present yet, but I'm doing my shopping at home.'

They were spending Christmas at Amy's parents'. Leela looked forward to it: as much to the warmth and adult conversation, the sense of an ordered world, as to the comfort.

'I'm feeling really sick, Leela,' said Amy pathetically.

'Get into bed,' she suggested. Amy climbed under the duvet.

'I'll get you some aspirin,' Leela said.

'Think I just need to sleep,' she said, rolling herself in the covers. 'Talk to me for a bit.'

Leela sat on the other side of the bed, hugging her knees, and they began a conversation; Amy fell asleep within minutes. The room filled with her smell: a mix of musk, tea, and yoghurt.

Leela went downstairs, feeling she was on a stage set, waiting to be found. The others knew she would be there, but only for a couple of days before she and Amy went away.

She opened her book, *Moon Park*. She was reading about cunnilingus in a lift when the door opened, introducing a man in a brown suit and loafers, James, and a blast of cold air.

'Hi Leela,' James said. He gave her a big grin. They hugged. 'How was your trip? Did you get in today?'

'In the afternoon.'

'Is Amy here?' James was getting a pouch of tobacco out of his jacket pocket. He put down a leather briefcase, sat in an armchair near Leela, and began to talk, rolling a cigarette. Tobacco fell on his corduroy suit. He worked in art publishing. How grown up everyone had become.

'How's work?' Leela asked.

James lit the cigarette. Smoke filtered into his blondish hair. 'Huh?' he said.

'How's work?'

'It's all right.' He grinned, showing yellow teeth. 'It's all right, it's all right.' He sighed, shoved his hand in his hair, smoked again. 'Actually it's good. They really like me.'

'Oh really? That's good.'

'Yeah, yeah,' James drawled. 'They get me to come along to a lot of important meetings, stuff I'm not even supposed to be at.'

'What's your actual job?'

She had to repeat the question because he was making for the kitchen. His shirt cuffs flared. His trousers were too long. His hair became dishevelled. He came back with three cans of lager from a four pack.

'Wannabeer?'

'No thanks. Um – okay.'

He was a marketing executive, it was his job to promote art books. But his art history degree and ability to talk to anyone had led to his getting to know the editorial department. Now they took him to meetings, and he'd met a professional art historian, and sat in on a meeting with another regular author.

'It's like a ceramic book. Like updated ceramics.'

'Oh right. My dad used to do pottery.'

'Not pottery. They're very particular. You're supposed to call them ceramicists.'

'Oh, really?'

'Yeah. It's like a really big deal for them.'

His mobile buzzed, and he waved it. Leela was slightly put out; everyone seemed to have a mobile now. 'Excuse me for a second.'

'Sure.'

There was a creaking on the stairs. Ellen came in. She was thinner than Leela remembered her. 'Let me just take a shower,' she said after she hugged Leela. 'I left here at seven this morning.' She worked in sales, and did shifts. She went to her room, and Leela, disenfranchised, went to see if Amy was up. She was; music blared from her stereo, she was brushing her hair, and putting on make-up. The honey and lemon Leela had made her was untouched.

'These pills Tom got me are fucking brilliant.'

Ellen's boyfriend had gone out to get her the cold remedy. It was now time for everyone to go to the pub on the main road.

Ellen, Tom, James, Amy and Leela sheltered in the front bar and drank pints, followed by whiskies. Tom's cheerful face became rosy. Amy became more and more amusing, and loud. She knocked over a drink. James's chat became more frenetic and less clearly enounced. The lights got brighter. Leela ate crisps. Amy licked the crumbs off the packet. The jukebox was turned off.

They went home.

In the dark, Amy whispered grievances. 'We all pay the same rent, right, but this is the worst room.'

'I think it's nice,' said Leela, partly out of loyalty, partly out of a desire not to have the conversation because her own resentment was more than she could handle; she preferred to pretend other people were more easy-going than she, and partly because she did think the room attractive. Admittedly it backed onto a yard and the small window was barred. But the room was big enough for a double bed, there was a fitted wardrobe, and it was possessed of the cosiness and comfort that Amy's rooms always had. Was it her friend's presence, or the props that travelled with her: a fringed lamp, a stereo, candles, a bedspread, a rug from home?

'Yeah, well, you should see James's room, or Tom's. It's because they found the house, and James said we'd get dibs on rooms, but he got one of the best ones, and so did Tom, and obviously they made sure Ellen did.'

How, Leela wondered, did she really feel about Simon? She longed to talk to Amy about him. She would when they were on the train. Perhaps he was her boyfriend. No. They were seeing each other. She felt a warm burst of affection for him, in his absence. It was sweet, he could be sweet. She had someone, that part of her life wasn't inactive. She fell asleep, the night getting away from her, carrying her like a soporific toddler towards sanity, breakfast, the pretence of function.

10

'What do you think?' Amy was whispering so loudly she almost seemed to be shouting.

'About what?'

'Oh, come on.'

'He's nice, he's nice looking,' Leela said. She felt thrilled, but put-upon.

'Did you talk to him?' Amy was singing out her words in aggressive exuberance. She dabbed powder on her face, stretched her mouth, reapplied lipstick. Leela looked at herself in the mirror, recoiled, wondered if the skin under her eyes could really be so dark.

'Pub mirrors are horrible, aren't they?'

'Ugh.'

They began to leave the lavatory.

'So are you going to pull him?'

'What?'

'Rob. Are you going to pull him?'

Leela felt rattled and became aggressive in turn. 'What are you on about? Leave me alone.'

'I'm just trying to help. Jesus.' Amy marched away, and a marooned Leela watched her. Without her friend, she was helpless.

Leela and Rob had a conversation. He was tall, dark-haired, fair-skinned, a bit awkward.

'So what do you do?' Leela asked abruptly. She had Simon after all, or whatever, she didn't need this. Nevertheless, Rob's attention, what she saw as his slightly rat-like smile, unnerved her. He continued to meet her eyes.

'I'm in gardening.'

'Right. Do you like that?'

He shrugged. 'It's all right. Pretty boring.' He grinned at her.

They were upstairs in the pub. Crowded: Christmas Eve. She and Amy had come up to Stratford the day before. That was when Leela had met Rob, the elder brother of Amy's chirpier, but less good-looking friend Jason, and a few of Amy's other numerous friends from home. Like Leela, perhaps like everyone, Amy had a different persona for college and for the town where she'd grown up. At home, many of her friends were the easy-going, down-to-earth young men she'd worked or drunk with: Jason and she had waited tables at the Grillhouse, a steak place in a retail park. Jason still worked there, and was now the junior manager. Amy hadn't met Rob, but had told Jason to bring his fit brother along. Rob was reputed to be serious. He and Leela sounded ideal for each other, in the short term.

They were standing up now, wedged against a small table with a stool near it. The stool was covered in coats. The pub was smoky. Leela shrank into the passage. Rob put an arm around her, just brushing her shoulder, as three men walked by. They skirted Leela and Rob as a couple.

'What about Simon?' Leela had checked with Amy when they were getting ready.

'Well, has he asked you to be his girlfriend?'

'No, but, I mean, we see each other almost every week. Sometimes more than once a week.'

'Has he had a conversation with you about seeing other people?'

'No.' Leela had felt sick.

Rob looked at her now and, as though straining a group of muscles, made a conversational foray. 'Have you been to Stratford before?'

Leela's heart sank. 'Yeah, a few times, yeah. To … visit Amy and stuff.'

'Oh, right.' He nodded. She examined his hair, which was impeccable with gel. Jason must have told him Amy had a friend who was single. Last night they'd smiled at each other; today Amy had reported that Jason said Rob thought Leela was fit. It was on, then.

'He's a nice-looking boy, love,' Amy's mother had remarked.

There they were. She smiled at Rob. He smiled uneasily back.

'I think I feel sick.'

'I feel really unwell. Here, do you want some cheese? Mm, so fattening and good.' Amy cut herself a piece of stilton and ate it. Leela removed orange peel from her sweater and lay prone on the sofa.

'We can do the Mr Motivator video tomorrow,' Amy said.

'That bloke in Lycra?'

'He's brilliant. It really tones you up.'

'Okay.'

They lay near the fire, and outside the lawn and garden darkened; late winter, Christmas Day. Leela was sand-wiched between the softness of the sofa and the hot blast of the fire and aware, further away, of the cold beyond the French doors. It was like *Jane Eyre*, she thought groggily, but without the cruelty. Surely they would now start read-ing enormous picture books, or look at maps, then fall into a frowsy and terrifying dream. England at Christmas was always like this: a fictional place into which she, Gulliver-like, had fallen. But Amy's family and their warmth cush-ioned her.

Orange peel, pips, and cheese rind sat on a plate. Leela and Amy drank tea.

'I'm seriously going to lose some weight.'

'Yeah, as soon as New Year's done.'

'So we'll be fat for New Year?'

'It's inevitable, with the way it comes straight after Christmas.' Amy pressed her stomach down and towards her groin, as though willing it to flatten.

'I feel sick,' Leela repeated.

'Cheese?'

They both started to laugh.

'Maybe just a bit.'

Leela went up to stash her presents, throw away the wrapping, and tidy up – they were later going out to the sole pub nearby that would be open, with Amy's father and a friend of his. Just then, the telephone began to ring. Amy's mother's silvery voice called up.

'Lee-la!'

'Yes?'

'Telephone for you, love. It's your mother.'

She ran down the stairs, slightly embarrassed. She'd given her parents the number when she had still been in Paris. But she'd half hoped they wouldn't call. She had a vague sense that Amy's parents disapproved of hers, but couldn't be sure. She felt mildly guilty about it, and shifty, as whenever different areas of her life converged.

'Hello?'

She held the cordless phone Amy's mother had given her, and stood looking at the dresser in the kitchen.

'Hello darling,' said her mother's voice, unexpectedly melodious and soft.

'Hi,' Leela repeated.

'Happy Christmas. We thought this'd be a good time to catch you. Are you having a good time?' Her voice, dissociated from her physical presence, was flexible and slightly cracked.

'Happy Christmas,' Leela said.

'So how is it?'

'It's nice, I'm having a really nice time.' She was, but her voice sounded flat and resentful.

In the hall she heard Amy and her little brother squabbling.

Later that night she and Amy lay in bed together, a habit from earlier in their friendship, and talked in the darkness.

'So has what's-his-name been in touch?'

'Simon?' Leela could tell she had her friend's attention. 'No. I don't really know what's happening.' She stretched out one bare foot and a pyjama'd leg. Amy in sleep was assertive about the covers. Leela usually tried the stealth pull: loosening the duvet from Amy's grasp, then rolling over to cover herself. It rarely worked for long.

'Did he speak to you before you left?'

'Well, we saw each other a few days before that.'

'Did he say when he'd be in touch?'

'Uh, no.'

'Oh, right.'

Silence.

'So you didn't fancy Rob?'

'He was fit, sort of. Do you think the lower half of his face is a bit ratty?'

'Well – no, I think he's lovely looking.'

'We didn't have anything to say to each other.'

'You didn't have to *say* anything.'

'Yeah. I dunno. I didn't want to. What did he say? Did he say anything?'

Amy rolled over, taking much of the duvet with her. 'Dunno. Jason said, Rob said he thought Leela fancied him, then she didn't get off with him.'

Leela mused on this. After a minute or two she said, 'But listen, right –'

Amy was asleep.

Leela lay with one leg under the covers, then got up and walked around. She went to the window and put her head under the heavy velvet curtain, a little away from the icy pane. Outside it was nearly dark, except for the acid-white glow of a street light. In the garden, the leaves of a small tree next to the wall appeared to be dead still.

She went back to bed, thinking wistfully for some reason of the discomfort of sleeping at Simon's. He never stayed at her house, of course; she thought of the platform bed and didn't miss it. She annexed part of the duvet, and rolled to the side, to avoid Amy, who was saying something indistinct and violent in sleep, and tossing from one side to the other.

LONDON

11

'Can we take it a bit shorter?'

The stylist put down the hand mirror. She looked annoyed. 'Shorter than that?'

'Yeah, a bit, yeah.'

'If I take it shorter it won't look *feminine*.' She seemed exasperated. This was the last appointment; Thursday nights there was a special offer.

'I want it shorter,' Leela said.

'I'll have to use clippers.'

'Fine.'

No one else was left in the salon. Its chrome fittings glinted in the night. The steam that lingered smelled vanilla, like hairspray, or teen perfume. Leela went into the cold, defiant but suspecting once again she'd done herself a bad turn.

She stood outside Amy's door ringing the bell and ignoring the waiters who came out of the Indian restaurant downstairs to smoke.

'Not there, ah?' said the waiter on the doorstep of the Bombay Tandoori.

'She is there,' Leela mumbled. 'We arranged. She – I –'

There was a heavy flurry down the stairs. The door shot open.

'Sorry! Come up. I just – aw!' Amy hugged Leela.

The waiter looked on with interest. The rain carried on falling, cold and sharp, just enough to make Leela's neck glow.

'Come in, come in, sorry, I was just on the phone to Mum.'

Leela followed as she ran up the stairs. At her door, Amy turned. 'Oh my god, your hair! Come inside. I'll get the kettle on.'

Leela sat on the broken futon and the rain rained. What if there were floods, and she had to stay here forever? She had a sudden urge to text Richard. She typed, 'Hi sweetie', then dropped the phone when Amy came back in.

'Do you hate it?'

'Well, gosh! It's short, isn't it? But it's cool! Very cool!' 'Cool' was a word Amy used to denote things that were foreign to her. She now used another. 'It looks really trendy.' She peered at Leela. 'It's very short, isn't it?'

Leela knelt on the futon so she could see herself in the mirror. She pushed her hair around. 'Do I look like a 1980s footballer?'

'No! Don't be silly. You look lovely. It's just –' Amy's eyes narrowed, and she darted back into the tiny kitchen to hasten out the tea bags, slop the tea, put in skimmed milk, and bring out the mugs.

'Can I have sugar?' Leela asked accusingly.

'Oh shit, sorry.' Amy went back into the kitchen and returned with an aged packet of caster sugar and a spoon. 'Here.' She plonked it next to Leela and turned up the music. She sang along, then turned it down, lit some candles, and sat next to Leela.

'It's just –?'

'It's just probably a good idea to, to, definitely wear make-up. And, you know, more skirts and stuff. Which you're doing anyway! You dress so much better than you did. What made you do it?'

Leela pushed bits of hair around to see if there were ways of looking more mysterious, less startled. 'I don't know. I'd been thinking about it. I thought it might feel lighter, it'd be fresh. Why not?'

'Do you think Richard'll like it?'

Leela sat down. 'Yeah,' she said. She caressed the near-shaven back of her head, and felt uneasy.

At some point in the night, Richard joined her in his bed; his cold hands and feet crept towards her legs. She flinched and withdrew. He chuckled and persisted.

'What time is it? Stop it, your hands are freezing.'

'I don't know, about two. We had to work late. The presentation's done though.'

He fell asleep soon. Leela lay watching a parallelogram of light, ugly, indifferent, from the road. Slowly it moved across the ceiling. She felt helpless against the threat of loneliness, and replayed part of her conversation with Amy.

The morning was both more and less frightening. Grey light came under the blinds; she made out the comforting shape of the large duvet, but the day was about to begin. She woke with Richard's hard-on tucked between her legs from behind. He sighed, and rocked closer as though to jog her memory. Leela tried to edge away. She craned her neck to look at the clock on the bedside table, but couldn't see it for his head.

'What time is it?'

'Come here.'

'I don't know if I –' The duvet, the room depressed her, but she would have liked to stay in bed for a long time, and get up after he'd left, as on days when the agency had no work for her and she sat in the flat, using the internet, reading, or writing things on pieces of printer paper. By mid-morning, all traces of him gone, she could wash up, tidy, then enjoy a sullen complicity with the furniture, and the blush-coloured carpet.

His fingers rooted about between her legs.

'Your nails –'

'Sorry sweetie, I'll trim them today.'

She tried not to think of the infection she'd had, which never showed up in tests, but reappeared to make her sore. She'd begun to simulate orgasms a while ago, she'd forgotten why; now she worried she couldn't remember how to come normally.

'I'm really turned on,' he said.

'Do you want me to go down on you?'

'Do you want to?'

'I can.'

'Not if you don't want to.'

'I want to.' She wanted to pretend the morning hadn't yet happened. She snaked under the duvet towards his crotch, and he began to masturbate and to palpate one of her breasts, eyes closed, while she stuck out her tongue. His fist accelerated; she moved back so it wouldn't hit her nose. Underneath the duvet, the air was warm and humid, a strange alternative world. When he came it was salty and viscous.

She resurfaced. He put an arm around her and kissed the top of her head. 'That was lovely.'

'Did you smoke yesterday?'

'Only half a sneaky fag outside the office. Could you smell it?'

'You taste different.'

She lay against the pillow, the padding of her sleep gone.

'I've got to have a shower, sweetie.' He got up, mock-groaning, and peeked through the blinds. 'Ugh, still raining.'

She watched him walk, tall, hairy, thin, out of the bedroom. Suddenly his head reappeared. 'Jesus. What have you done to your hair?'

Leela watched his expression. 'I cut it.'

'Yesterday?' He came closer.

She turned to show him the nape. 'I like the back.'

'The back's nice.' He stood, irresolute and naked, a towel in his hand.

'It's my hair.'

'It makes your shoulders look nice,' he said. 'I've got to get ready.'

Leela, unbreakfasted, opened her bag. Yes. Lurking at the bottom, with a couple of wrapped tampons and one glove, was a slim dark chocolate wrapped in cellophane. 'Merci,' said the label in faux-cute serif font. Richard's ex-girlfriend had left them for him on a visit. Leela had mocked the name; she ate the chocolates with cannibalistic satisfaction when she was hungry, which was often. Richard ate irregularly, though he ate well, and his fridge was full of things Leela didn't consider food, like smoked cheese and salami.

The phone call came when she was returning from the park at the end of her lunch hour.

'Hi sweetie!'

'Hi sweetie,' he responded. 'Listen, I've had an email from Dad.'

She took the news well, stopped in the doorway of a shop, and had to move aside when young men came out with cigarettes and bottles of Lucozade. Friday, the end of the week.

'When's he here? How many days?'

Richard's father lived in Germany. He owned the flat where his son and, unofficially, Leela lived. He would be coming to London on work the following afternoon, and staying for a few days. Leela would have to gather her things and take them back to her house.

She didn't say, 'Are you going to tell him about me?'

Richard had a strange relationship with his father. Typically, when he and Leela fought about his not having disclosed Leela's existence, he would say, 'I'm not even that close to him. There are a lot of things I don't tell him.'

But Leela suspected he enjoyed the time away from her and with his father, out to nice dinners and strolling around exhibitions. She had more or less moved in with him, and abandoned the daily carrying of a change of clothes, toothbrush, hairbrush etc with her to work, then out, then back to his house. She wanted to be settled; she didn't want to have to think so often about the small objects that supported her life.

In the afternoon, while the rest of the office grew skittish after a Friday lunch in the pub and sent round droll email forwards, she brooded on those objects. Her hairdryer. Her underwear. Socks, tights, clothes, superannuated make-up, shoes, trainers, a disposable camera that wasn't yet ready to be disposed of. She dreamed of having few possessions. But it would be the usual degrading scramble of things stuffed in supermarket plastic bags, and Richard, probably, left holding out to her a pair of knickers that had fallen from one of them.

'Come home and I'll cook you a nice dinner tonight,' he said at the end of the call.

'It's not my fucking home, is it.'

She left work, disregarding the injunctions from her temporary colleagues to have a good weekend. Was a weekend not merely an opportunity to have long, unfurling arguments and dilatory sex; to spend a long time apologising for things one had said, and a shorter time in the warmth of apparent forgiveness?

On the tube, she was distracted by the profusion of stuff. She tried to read the magazine she'd bought, and scanned the pictures of things with alluring, slightly threatening legends: Pointy-toed boots, Dune, £49.99. Should she wear different nail polish? Change her eye make-up?

She surfed, too, the body parts around her. One day, in bed, Richard had said that when he looked at women it wasn't in the way she had feared. Or rather, that her fears weren't sufficiently comprehensive. 'It's not necessarily just someone who looks really beautiful,' he said. 'Half the time, I'm looking at their clothes, or how they've put together a look.'

'But not all the time.'

He'd giggled, perhaps at his own audacity. 'When you look in a more sexual way, I suppose there's an element of looking at individual body parts. Sometimes you see a great arse, or a nice pair of breasts. You're not really looking at the person as a whole.'

One cold afternoon, when she was in between jobs, Leela had gone to her house and surfed porn on her flatmate Jon's computer. The images of women with exaggerated breasts, tans, and open orifices presented to the viewer had aroused her, but in a way she found embarrassing, as though she'd protested a lack of hunger, then, pressed to eat junk food, overeaten anyway. There was no elegance to this desire.

Still, since that conversation, she'd found herself trying to replicate Richard's ruthless gaze; in public places, she let her eyes rifle women's bodies. Breasts? A bit saggy. Bum? Large. But the girl over there had buttocks that rose in a high curve like those in underwear advertisements. She now turned, as though subliminally aware of Leela's thoughts, and gave Leela a hard look. Leela, embarrassed, turned away. The tube thundered through its endless tunnel.

'Hi sweetie.' Tall, friendly, he opened the door for her, ran a hand through his hair, smiled. Leela leaned across for a kiss. She was seething.

'How was the day?' she asked.

'Good. I thought I wouldn't get off early but I did. We've submitted the presentation, so they've got to get back to us.'

'Great.'

She followed him to the kitchen.

'Do you want a drink?'

'Mm.' She put down her bag. 'I'm thinking I'll pack and get to my place tonight.'

'Oh, really? Dad isn't getting here till around lunchtime tomorrow.'

'Yeah, but, whatever, it'd be nice to wake up at home, have the day.'

'Okay.'

Glass in hand, she went to the bedroom and began to take clothes out of her drawer.

Richard appeared in the doorway, hand in hair. 'I could put some stuff in the spare room under the bed if you want.'

Leela, on her knees amid a collection of Tesco bags, ground her teeth. 'Why?'

'If you don't want to carry it all back.'

'Oh, I think it's simpler.' She stuffed the errant leg of a pair of tights into another bag, and began to carry several of them towards the hall.

'You don't have to go tonight,' Richard repeated.

'I'd rather.' She turned on her heel and went back towards the bags.

'Okay.'

They sat with plates of saffron risotto in tiny servings. Leela drank more, and poured more wine into Richard's glass, then into her own. She didn't care, anyway. The wine's taste altered; from dry and reminiscent of lemons, it became sourer. Richard went to the kitchen to get the next dish, skate with capers and tomatoes. They'd eaten something similar in France in the summer, when they'd gone to the wedding of one of his friends. The bride had asked Leela if she and Richard planned to marry.

'I don't know if he wants to,' Leela had said.

Catherine had looked at her directly, and tucked her blonde hair behind her ear. 'Set yourself a time limit,' she advised. 'I did that with Tom. I told myself, three years and you're out. By the time he asked me, I was mentally dividing up our furniture.'

Leela had laughed, but the conversation had stayed with her.

'Why can't we just move in together?' she now asked Richard for the millionth time.

He grinned. 'We basically do live together.'

'But this isn't my space', a term he favoured, as in, "I like what you've done with this space".

'You have your stuff here.'

'I have to move out when your dad's here.'

'He's hardly ever here.'

'That's not the point.'

They sat down with the fish, which was excellently cooked.

'The fish is nice,' Leela said.

Richard looked troubled.

'What?'

'I feel like you're never satisfied.'

'What?' She felt apprehension mixed with the usual rage.

'You're never grateful.'

'*What?*'

'I think you should think about all the things I do for you,' he said doggedly.

'What about all the things I do for you?'

He looked doubtful, in the slightly aquiline way only a thin person with a long nose can. 'My point is, you only look at the things that upset you,' he said. 'I think you should look at all the things I do that are nice. Like cooking for you.'

'Practically speaking I cook for you more often.'

'You virtually live here.'

'Is that supposed to be some sort of favour?' She shot up from the sofa.

'Well,' he said, quietly indignant, 'you probably have a better lifestyle than you otherwise would because of it.'

'What's wrong with my *lifestyle*?'

'This flat. It's nicer than yours.'

'There's nothing wrong with my flat. At least I don't have to shunt out of it every time your dad comes to town.'

He folded his arms. The oval glass table, which he'd coveted for weeks before he bought it from the antiques market, stood between them like a punctuation mark.

'Oh, hi. I thought I heard you come in last night.' Jon walked past a still-sleeping Leela, fumbling for the coffee powder in the kitchen, and opened the fridge. The phone began to ring. He bounded out. 'Jesus! More people trying to sell me something.'

It struck Leela that these calls were the result of marketing strategies like those Richard and his colleagues put in place, with much plying of PowerPoint, for their clients. Jon, she heard, was having an animated conversation.

'No, he's not. He's away. Where? Uh … he's skiing. Yes. Well, in Colorado. It's a different season there.'

Leela grinned.

'But what's it about?' Jon enquired tensely, a man on the scent of a falsehood.

The kettle boiled. Leela tipped a small mountain of coffee into her individual-sized cafetière. A bird sang outside. The day was grey.

'Okay, I'll tell him, but he's pretty fucking acute, yeah?' Jon ended. Leela giggled, spilling coffee powder. The kitchen needed cleaning.

'Did you mean "astute"?'

'Thank you,' said Jon reprovingly. He took the kettle from her and poured hot water into a mug containing a single round tea bag. Immediately the water became dark and rank-smelling.

Leela sat on the counter, rubbing her eyes and waiting for coffee powder and water to turn into coffee.

'Time for a drastic change?' Jon said.

She started. His face was innocent of anything sly.

There was a long pause. Leela ran a hand through her short hair. 'Oh. You mean the hair. Yeah – dunno. It seemed like a good idea.'

'Well, it'll grow,' Jon pointed out. He looked at her again, as though deciding whether to speak. 'So Richard's away?'

Leela felt herself blush. 'His dad's here, so he's spending time with him.' She wondered if she'd left any of her plastic bags in the hall.

Jon nodded, and smiled at her. He stopped stirring his tea, and went back to his room.

Leela spent a quiet day, each part unfolding with tedious languor. She regarded the bags she'd deposited in her room, and considered unpacking. She cleaned the bath. She went to the small supermarket on the High Road, and bought avocadoes, bread, butter, lemons, coffee, milk, cereal. She came home and put away the food. She phoned Amy.

'It's not so much that I miss him. It's that I resent that he doesn't miss me.'

'Maybe he's just not as insecure as you.'

Leela brooded. She sipped her tea. 'Can I have sugar?'

'Oh, sorry. It's in the kitchen.'

Amy was often free at weekends, because the man she was seeing was attached. Leela, however, was usually busy, having an absorbing, miserable weekend of social engagements, arguing, and sex, with the odd good meal thrown in.

'Do you actually want to spend all your time with him?' Amy asked.

'No. I just feel better when he's there.'

Richard usually took Leela along when he met his friends. 'There's nothing I'd say to them if you weren't here that I wouldn't say when you are,' he said. As if in retribution, he tended to come along whenever Leela met a friend; this went down badly with her friends.

She put in the sugar, stirred it, went to the mirror over the mantelpiece to check how her hair looked today, then turned away before she looked. 'How are things going with Andrew, anyway?'

Amy made a face. 'He's away for the weekend, with Laura.'

When she was on her way home, Richard called. She listened to the message as she walked from the tube to her house, through the shadows of trees and other houses on the back street.

Richard's voice was warm, slightly hesitant. 'Hi sweetie, it's me. I'm sorry we parted on a bad note. Give me a ring if you get this soon. Otherwise, talk to you tomorrow. And Dad's out for a bit in the afternoon so we could meet up if you want. Anyway, hope you had a good day, and speak to you soon.'

Leela looked at the screen of her phone. It was almost an hour since his call. The message sat in her heart like ballast, something to be held against the vast flow of indifference, time, transience. He had called. In the moment of freedom from her usual sense of lack, she felt she could do anything: tell him it was over, be alone. She wouldn't call now, she'd call back tomorrow. She remembered, too, as she let herself into the darkened hall of her house – a place she now considered home but which she'd pass through just as she'd passed through other rented accommodation, other rooms, and made conversation with other flatmates – the time Richard had called her over when his father had last been in town. Richard had moved to the spare room, which had a single bed. They had repaired there, and begun to kiss: he had coaxed Leela into bed. It had struck her that he'd invited her over for an hour so they could have sex and that this was – was it? – an insulting way to treat her. She'd submitted, completely callously, closed her eyes, and thought without guilt of anonymous bodies, large-breasted women, images from pornography: dark, hot openings. She'd come silently and with satisfaction. Afterwards, Richard had said, 'You felt slightly absent during sex.'

'What makes you say that?' she'd asked.

'You weren't completely engaged. I don't think that's fair. I don't think you'd like it if I did that.'

But he did make love with his eyes closed, and she was reasonably sure he thought not of her but of other people, and other images as he moved. Did she care? Occasionally she realised she was more detached from the experience than she admitted. Didn't she, too, think of other things, other pictures, animated by the desire of other, unseen but multiple people?

She closed the door, leaving behind her the shifting panel of light from the street that came through the stained glass. She went towards her bedroom to get a towel. She'd shower, wash her hair, dry it, put some gunk in it, so she wouldn't make herself even later in the morning. On her way to work she would, she thought, call Richard, and apologise for the things she'd said.

12

Installed at her desk at ten past nine, relieved that she wasn't later, then depressed to be there at all, Leela went into a reverie.

It was bizarre to think it had only been a year ago, in May, that she'd been considering whether to stay in Paris a second year. There was a simple application process by which teachers had to submit a letter asking to renew their contracts. Nina was going to stay, but Kate wasn't. Leela had debated the question with herself. She made lists, on foolscap copies, under two columns: Pros and Cons. The lists ran overleaf. She wore a frown. One day, towards the end of the month, in blithe sunshine, she went for a walk towards the Left Bank.

The lists danced in her head. Paris seemed unreal, or was it she who was without substance? A man bumped into her, and apologised furtively. On the boulevard, the trees were new in leaf. Near Les Halles, stalls bristled with sunglasses in coloured frames. The sun hit the top of the Tour Saint Jacques and shattered everywhere.

She crossed bridge after bridge, then took a long stroll home as the sun went in. She walked through the new Louvre, whose neoclassical courts frightened her. She would apply to renew her post, she decided. Paris was Paris: she had not yet had enough of it. There would be other encounters, adventures perhaps. She sat on a bench near the river and wondered where Patrick was these days: maybe in his flat, maybe returned to England. They had reached a mutual truce and agreed, silently, to forget each other's existence, after the episode in January when Leela had gone to see him and, intending to mention dryly and in passing the results (none) of her liaison with Simon, had instead laid out, in rage, all the misdemeanours Patrick's friend had made and the ways in which his treatment of her, Leela, had been tawdry and unsatisfactory (unreturned messages, a general disappearance, but once, when she'd run into him on the street, an annoyingly bluff chat terminating in a kiss and a suggestion they 'go for a drink sometime'). Patrick had listened, become more and more politely detached, smoked in silence, then got up, paced about a bit, and suggested it had been Leela's fault. What had she expected?

'Why didn't you tell me what he was like?' she burst out. His eyebrows had shot up; she'd gone too far.

Now they lived in the same city, or didn't, and she worked ten minutes from his apartment, and went out in the same area, but in other streets, other bars, and they didn't see each other.

She went home and wrote the letter asking to have her contract renewed.

The next day, when she went to the school office to drop it off, Mme Sarraute shrugged and said applications had officially closed, and, anyway, there had been several excellent candidates from outside the school. It was hardly worth Leela's putting in her letter.

She could have insisted, or spoken to the director of teaching. Instead, she took the letter home, cried a single tear, and crumpled it.

That Sunday, the first of June, she went for another walk along the bridges of Paris, fictional in their loveliness, heedless in their eternity, and the sunshine in which she walked seemed to erase her as she passed through it.

Nine forty. There were three, perhaps more, hours till lunch, when she would tramp through the next-door shopping mall, which was furnished with further fluorescent light and clothes in mixes of man-made fibres, plastic jewellery, make-up, hair products.

Gemma, a blonde girl with a triangular smile, was one of the senior administrators in the office where Leela was filling in as Junior Administrative Secretary to Mike Pringle, a man with a beard who took Leela's job alarmingly seriously. Gemma liked the place where they worked. There was a corporate discount at the Canary Wharf branch of Fitness First, she told Leela, in Leela's first week.

'Great.'

'It's a really good gym.' She fixed Leela in the eye. 'They have elliptical trainers, treadmills, an aerobics studio. *Yoga*, if that's what you're into.'

'Great.'

Yesterday Gemma had come back from lunch carrying a plastic bag, and plopped it on Leela's desk. 'Look, I got a whole ton of Redken shampoos.'

'Really?' Leela had no idea what these were, and was in the middle of filling in her time sheet to claim she had been away from her desk for half an hour when it had in fact been an hour and ten minutes.

'Yeah.' Gemma bristled with pleasure. 'I thought I'd treat myself for working so hard.'

Leela smiled. 'Sounds like a good idea.'

She had been in the fluorescent light of the office, then the mall, for too long.

On the tube, she brooded. Everything in the office conspired against her; even the physical environment. The dull grey low-pile carpet, with its near-imperceptible pattern of blue squares arranged in diagonals; the grey and black desk chairs; the counterfeit wooden tables. The pens were useless yellow ballpoints, the pencils had smudgy erasers. Even the files she was supposed to keep in order – sometimes she did, at other times she shoved 'Claims Ranked by Order [Mortality]' into a totally different section, like 'Mortality [Isle of Wight]' – came in different colours: red, blue, yellow, green, but depressing tones of those colours. Yellow was a dirty mustard, red a faded maroon, blue a slatey mess, green resembled ageing Astroturf.

By summer she was getting up early to go to the gym before work. Richard was just waking when she left the flat to walk to the tube, under trees in yellow-green leaf. When she got there, she clutched her card, feeling a mix of assurance – she did the same workout every day – and slight nerves. The presence of other people gave the gym an odd sense of theatre.

The lights were bright, fluorescent. She felt the nervous energy of morning coffee give way to sweat, and the body took over from the mind, endlessly iterating the same action.

A dance song played, a pumping beat; the legs worked harder. Next to her, a very thin, tanned blonde woman stepped much faster than Leela. She was using one of the older, more resistant stair machines. She arrived every day before the eight o'clock rush and stayed, with silent determination, on the machine for twenty minutes. She wore sports leggings and a crop top between which her midriff was nearly flat, a yellowish colour. Leela had watched her on many days. She seemed to work by the calorie counter on the machine, and burnt off at least a thousand calories as she moved between the stepper, the treadmill, and the elliptical trainer. When she arrived, she had a slight exoform curve to her belly; by the time she was well into her workout and an exhausted Leela was heading to the changing room, any sign of fullness was gone. She probably aimed to burn off every calorie she had consumed the previous day. In this way her balance with the world remained at nil: she might just as well have not been there.

After lunch Leela fished out her notebook. Near the end, she had written the numbers from one to a hundred, each above a small box. In some of the boxes she'd drawn a symbol denoting a smiling face; in others, the box had been coloured black. It was rare for there to be a line of smiles longer than four or five; there was one stretch of eleven but, she thought, the black squares that followed it probably ought to have swallowed half the page.

Today's square was still blank. Nothing had happened; she had risen early, given Richard a kiss, smiled at him as he made sleepily for the bathroom while she was on her way out, and she had gone to the gym. The tension that always seemed to buzz between her neck and shoulders, and which resulted either in tears or bitten-out words of anger, had been allowed to dissipate somewhere between the stair climber and the scent of the gym's shower gel, a generic green smell that might have been called Alpine Fresh, or Forest Morning.

The secret, strange ways her day passed, her frustrations when the photocopier kept jamming, and she had to produce reduced-size, double-sided copies of annotated documents for Mike to take away with him on a business trip, and it was after five thirty and everyone else had left, and she fretted about how long the tube journey back would take, were things she tried to tell Richard about. He sympathised, but she knew he didn't understand.

She stared at today's blank square.

'If we could just have a while without arguing,' he had said, head in hands. 'I hate it when we argue.'

Leela's jaw had begun to ache. They had been sitting on his sofa on a Sunday night, the sky outside black. The weekend had passed in the usual way: late-night arguing, matinal apologies, interminable resentment.

She said nothing for a bit. 'You want us not to disagree?'

'Not that, but not have these horrible arguments.'

She considered it coldly. There had been other things that had frightened her, but which she had dealt with: final exams, or moving to a new city. This too could be done.

'Are you angry?' he enquired apprehensively. It was their pattern: when she became self-sufficient, he would break her down with affection or argument till the usual imbalance was restored.

'Not at all,' she said. Later, when he was on the phone, she drew the set of squares, crazy in their alignment, each row tilting hopefully upwards.

After that, her zeal for achieving, in a new but similar way to the meaningless achievements of the gym, made her manage to be pleasant and, at worst, a little withdrawn for ten days. They had a spat one Saturday at a party when Richard allowed a dull and not very attractive woman to flirt with him, while a silent, increasingly enraged Leela looked on; he then tried to talk to Leela's friend's very attractive girlfriend before she drunkenly disappeared to the bathroom. 'You always get paranoid when I talk to anyone more beautiful than you,' he observed. They had a teary row on the road towards her house; he grabbed her satchel and slung it over a wall into the garden of a block of council flats.

He climbed over the wall, and returned with the satchel, and they continued up the road in sullen silence, but she ended up apologising the next day. On Monday, her bitterness at the usual betrayals – his, of her; hers, of herself – were compounded by having to record a black square in the note-book. She coloured it in with grim satisfaction – for a part of her was not sorry that the initiatives to control it had failed.

13

'What are you doing today?' Richard asked. For a moment, she saw him as he was – tall, slightly geeky, pleased to see her. She was so used to viewing him as the author of all her disappointment and frustration.

'I'll ring the agency. But I've got to fill out my tax return as well. I wonder if I'll find all the papers. Nightmare.'

The morning was pretty. Through the streaky kitchen window, sun flooded; the water-stained steel sink was bright.

'I don't have anything to do,' he mused.

'How do you mean?'

'Well, Javier's on leave, the proposal's with the client. Clara said she might not come in.'

'Oh, right.' She agitated the cafetière and plunged it. She poured carefully into a white bone china mug. Things always had to be a certain way in Richard's house.

'I suppose I could work from home,' he said. He chuckled.

'Huh?'

'We could hang out for a while, have a picnic or something.'

On the way from the deli, his hair blew across his face. He looked younger, more defenceless than when he was dressed for work; he wore a baggy shirt with flowers climbing over it in faded rows.

They stopped at the small park halfway up the road.

'What about here?'

'Isn't this for kids?'

'But there aren't any here.'

She followed him. They sat on mushroom-shaped stools amid the wood chippings, under the pleasant leaves of early summer.

'Do you want some olives?'

He ate half a sandwich, in sunflower-seed bread. He grinned at her with satisfaction and she, eating the other half, fingers slippery with oil from the sun-dried tomatoes, smiled too. She leaned back. The springy stool allowed her to look up and behind; only a few leaves were between her and the blue sky.

'It's going to be summer.'

'It is summer.'

'Late May?'

'Pretty much. We'll have a few warm days then it'll be over anyway.'

'That's true.' She sighed.

'Try the cheese.'

She passed him the lemonade. 'No, I'm full.'

'Sure?'

She nodded resignedly.

Leela texted Amy: So are we still on for today?

Amy: Yes! But Andrew won't be free till slightly later. Is that okay?

Leela, heart sinking: When?

Amy: About 8.30. We could meet a bit before, if I get done with work.

It was the middle of an uninspiring week. The date had been set up on Sunday – Amy had rung, Leela hadn't picked up, then Amy had left a teary-sounding message. Weekends were difficult for her, and Leela sometimes avoided the resentful telephone calls that Sundays brought. She rang back, and Amy asked her to come for a drink and meet Andrew.

'He's definitely going to be there, he's got a meeting before that, he's definitely staying over on Wednesday.'

She often sounded angry when she talked about him.

'Right, okay. Wednesday?' Leela said. She rolled her eyes at Richard, who was reading a magazine in the background. She raised her eyebrows; he nodded.

Now, she sighed. She'd have to hang around in town and wait for Andrew to be done with his meeting. Amy, she had a hunch, wouldn't appear much before. Richard had gone to see a school friend in Hampstead, at the flat he shared with his girlfriend. Leela had a mild pang. Not because the girlfriend was particularly attractive, but because Richard went to see them from time to time, when Leela happened to be busy, probably because there was a freedom and simplicity in their company that her presence would have impaired.

She wandered around the centre of London, killing time, and remembered again how pointless and depressing areas like Leicester Square were. Finally Amy rang. There turned out to have been a missed call.

'Where *are* you?' Amy's well-bred tones enquired.

'In Leicester Square, waiting,' said an irritated Leela.

'What are you doing there? We're here.'

'Where's here?'

'In the pub. On Whitehall. Get here when you can.'

She had a silent, sarcastic conversation with Amy on her walk past lit-up late-evening windows and hurrying figures. There was a shadow in the sky as it darkened; a wind blew dust.

Turning into the door of the pub, she left behind an emanation of the city – traffic fumes but also a scent of summer, perhaps from trees coming into flower somewhere near the Mall. She went into the classic atmosphere of a pub in London: carpet spray, crisps, smoke, beer, damp suiting.

Inside she became lost amid the repeated motifs of overcoats and work shirts, pink and blue and white, the features above them as alien as the clothing. Fucking drones, she thought, but was intimidated by their raw, pink faces.

She saw an attractive young woman, then a man's shoulder – his back was to her, he had close-cut grey hair. He leant into the girl, and she laughed. Leela's first impression was of her charisma; then the woman waved and the world slid into focus and became unforeign. It was Amy.

'Leela!' she cried.

'Hi,' said Leela, diffident, moving closer, but unable to help grinning as her friend, like a toddler, threw up her arms for a hug. Leela kissed her on the cheek.

'Good to see you!' said Amy, an utterance both formal and heartfelt that reminded Leela of Amy's father.

'Hi,' she said again, so aware of being the new arrival that it was hard to look at Andrew properly. Now she saw the cropped silver hair and blue eyes she recognised vaguely from TV. 'I'm Leela.'

'Hi Leela, great to meet you. Look, let me get you both a drink. Darling, another glass of wine?'

'That'd be lovely,' Amy said. She beamed. Leela was taken aback.

'Leela, what'll you have?'

'I'll get it.'

'No, absolutely not.'

'Um, a gin and tonic please.'

Amy was still beaming. Leela sat next to her, ran a hand through her hair, which was growing in unruly ways, and took in the table: Andrew's mobile; Amy's wallet; a near-empty glass of white wine, and an empty pint glass. She picked up a beer mat and put it down again; it was damp.

'He seems really nice,' Leela said. She knew Amy believed her to be hostile to the relationship and wanted her friend to be happy, or continue to be happy.

She began to hear murmurs of the chat around them.

'Ha ha ha! You fucking idiot!' An Australian accent. Someone thrust out his elbow; Leela moved her stool. Someone else laughed. A few tables away was a throng of standing people.

'Oh yeah, Andrew has amazing manners. Obviously. You won't have to go to the bar all night,' Amy said. Leela felt slightly diminished, embarrassed as well as aggrieved, as though she'd either desperately wanted to be there or to consume drinks paid for by Andrew. Where would she have been if she hadn't been here? At Richard's, perhaps, with a magazine and a takeaway while he was out, or angry with him, looking at the time, or at her house, either absorbed in something or discontented; she couldn't decide which.

Andrew was back. 'There's a booth over in the other side, shall we go there?' he asked. They picked up their stuff and followed him.

The side room, behind panelled screens, was nicer. The people who had been in the booth were leaving; they waited, then slid in, Amy in the corner, and Leela opposite. In the snug she felt less antagonised.

'Leela, Amy tells me you're a great reader,' Andrew said. 'I've been rereading lately, *Our Mutual Friend*. Do you know it?'

'Yeah, of course.'

'Is this Dickens? Am I wrong?' Amy's clear voice cut in.

Leela grinned at her.

'The descriptions at the beginning – the river, and London. It's amazing. I'd forgotten it completely, I now realise.'

'What did you do at university? I mean, what did you read?'

'English.' He smiled at her.

'Oh, really?'

He nodded, his face eager. 'It stays with you, you know. The love of books, and the things you learn about how to read. You lose the knowledge, or at least I have. Terrible verbal memory. I can't quote anything I read more than a week ago.' He grimaced.

'I know, me too,' Leela said.

'What are you reading right now?'

'I'm in between stuff,' she said. She was finding it hard to face a book; she subsisted on magazines, weekend supplements, and the internet. Now, she had a sudden enthusiasm for going to a second-hand bookshop. 'I decided I had too many books,' she went on. 'I thought I should stop buying them for a while.'

Andrew smiled. It was a smile of great flexibility and understanding. 'Ah, but books,' he said.

'Books are things too,' said Leela, without believing it.

His azure eyes softened. He smiled as though he had enough grace not to believe she meant it either.

Leela got into bed.

Richard kissed her. 'How was the evening?'

'Really nice actually.' Her voice was warm.

'Really?' He looked up from the book.

'Yeah, I really liked him.'

'Really?'

'He's great. I think he might be amazing for Amy.'

'Even though he's married?'

'It was weird,' Leela said. 'He mentioned his wife at one point – really naturally. I thought I'd hate him for it, but it made me feel he was less of a bastard. I do think he really cares about Amy.'

Richard looked at her for a little longer. 'You really liked him, didn't you?'

'Yeah,' said Leela slowly. 'I did. I was surprised.'

At Trafalgar Square, when she'd left them to go for her bus, Amy had hugged her, and Andrew kissed her on the cheek. 'It's really great to have met you, Leela,' he said. 'Really nice to talk, and I know how important you both are,' he looked at the two women, 'to each other.'

'Leela's my best friend!' said a slightly drunk Amy. Leela grinned. 'That's big shit!' Amy pointed out.

'It is big shit,' Andrew agreed, with only a little irony.

Leela half turned when she'd gone a few paces. The others were talking intently, and Andrew's arm was around Amy. She drew her cardigan about her, and wished she had a scarf; it wasn't that warm at night.

Now, as Richard continued to read his book on marketing techniques, she lay back, one arm under her head, and listened to the traffic pass outside the partly open window. Summer was coming, that was plain, but it wasn't here yet. She looked at Richard, reading, and pinching his earlobe, as he always did when concentrating. She thought of Andrew, his infinitely understanding smile, and his warmth; of Amy, and her reckless happiness; and she was aware, too, of the room around her, its artifices, the rustle of the duvet cover, and the almost animal sound of the occasional car on the road.

14

'Sweetie, are you ready?' Her voice was getting an edge. Early July, a Sunday evening. She had not gone to the gym; he had spent part of the afternoon on the telephone, just as they'd been about to go out to the flea market together, and she had begun to read but not been able to; a small argument, a make up, a stint in bed, and she was wondering with irritation where the time had gone.

Richard was ironing a shirt.

'I'll just be a couple of minutes,' he said, grinning at her.

Leela went and looked at herself in the mirror. Her hair was growing out, and she had put some stuff in it. She'd put on eyeliner, and a dress she liked.

She turned again. Richard was painstakingly ironing the back of the left sleeve.

'You're only going to put a jumper over it anyway,' she said.

'But I might take the jumper off inside.'

The figure in the mirror turned away from itself in exasperation. It folded its arms; the shoulders went up, towards the ears.

An hour later, out of the tube, they walked for a long time around a small area, repeatedly consulting the A–Z.

'Shit, we should have brought something,' Leela said. She was feeling uneasy. 'We're really late.'

They were near a dark square. She was suddenly filled with rage, and tears. 'Why couldn't you iron your fucking shirt earlier?' Her hands balled up; she began to cry.

Forty-five minutes later, they got to Ellen's door. It was open, the party had spilled into the corridor. Richard was smiling; he held a bottle of wine. Leela felt shaken. She was smiling too – she didn't know what she was feeling: hatred, fear, or merely the hope of release.

'Leela!' Amy grabbed them as soon as they came in. Leela got caught, to her surprise, saying hello to smiling, diffident Doug, an ex-boyfriend of Amy's: they'd been in a play together in their first year at college. Amy grabbed Richard's arm and began to have an intent conversation with him, still holding his arm, which irritated Leela, who remembered Amy pinning her to the wall of a women's toilet and hissing 'Stop flirting with Doug!' Leela had been baffled; she hadn't even been attracted to Doug, who equally certainly wasn't interested in her.

Doug was saying something: he brought over a blonde Canadian girl who was his girlfriend, and Leela, thinking the other woman was sweet, talked to her for a while.

Amy grabbed Leela's arm and dragged her outside. 'Stop being so fucking disloyal!'

'What are you talking about?'

'Stop talking to that bitch!'

'Why's she a bitch?'

'Fucking blonde, blondie, blonde bitch!' said Amy.

'You're ratted.'

'Yeah yeah, whatever. The point is, you shouldn't have been talking to her.'

'But why? You don't still care about Doug.'

'That's not the point. He rejected me, he rejected me.'

'I'm going inside.'

'No!'

'What about Andrew?' Leela tried.

'Andrew's obviously much better than Doug. Obviously. He's like a nine or *ten*, and Doug's a six. But,' and Amy's voice rose, 'he's *married*, right, so whassthepoint? Whassthepoint of it all? And anyway, you're my best friend.' Her hand tightened around Leela's arm. Some of the girls on the balcony looked at them and grinned.

'Look, another thing,' Leela said. 'Why were you flirting with Richard?' She had to repeat herself.

'Oh, don't be absurd,' Amy said.

Leela shivered. It wasn't warm. 'You kept touching his arm. You wouldn't have liked it if I'd done that. Remember the time you accused me of flirting with Doug?' Boring Doug, she appended silently.

Amy bent close and spoke loudly. 'Leela, I'm not interested in Richard.'

'All right!'

'I'd never flirt with your boyfriend.'

'All right, all right,' said Leela, now wondering where he was. 'Let's go back in.'

'Give me a hug!'

Leela allowed herself to be tightly held. Amy nearly unbalanced her. 'Let's go back inside. Let's get a drink.'

Leela watched her head towards the kitchen; on the way she was stopped by three different people who cried her name and whom she hugged and paused to talk to.

The party was full of yellow light, of chatter heard around a corner, of laughter, of music turned on and off, up and down, vaguely familiar faces, and girls who were well dressed, potential enemies: sometimes she felt there was an army of attractive women, agents of which kept appearing in her field of vision when she was out with Richard. The apparently unattractive, uninteresting girl was also to be feared, because she might be a double bluff. There was only one of Leela but many of the others. Sometimes she longed to acknowledge defeat. Richard was across the room now, smiling and talking to a pretty girl. She would give it a few minutes, then go over and say hello.

A long time later, when Richard was drunk enough, he agreed to go home. Leela had, by superhuman effort, reappeared only once in a while to find out who he was talking to – assorted girls, then, for a brief respite, a man, but who turned out to have a beautiful girlfriend who came to talk to Richard at length. Leela had said she wanted to go; Richard had smiled and said calmly, 'Maybe one more drink.' Forty minutes later, he was done. It struck Leela that she'd spent the last five hours feeling under threat; and this was a party she'd wanted to go to.

Amy reappeared. 'Leela, are you leaving? I want to leave too.'

Richard telephoned a cab and they went down to wait. When it appeared, Amy sat in the middle. She burst into tears.

'What's the matter?' Leela asked. She felt sorry for Amy, but also exasperated, and fearful too: Richard would judge her for how well she responded to this crisis. Worse, he might find Amy attractive amid it. What if he fantasised about her?

'Oh, it's just, oh, oh,' Amy cried. She put her hands to her face and sobbed. The taxi drove through dark east London streets. She continued to cry loudly, smeared her hands across her face, and sniffed. 'Oh, it was just seeing Doug.'

'Doug?'

'I liked him so much, and he doesn't like me at all, and – oh, it was just awful.'

They arrived at Amy's flat. Leela gave the driver instructions about where to stop. Suddenly Amy turned to her. 'Come and stay at mine. Please,' she said.

'What?'

'Please, please.' She begged with her whole body.

Leela's imagination briefly saw her doing the right thing. 'But I want to go back to Richard's,' she said.

'Please Leela.'

Richard said politely, 'Amy, you're more than welcome to come to mine.'

'No, I don't want to, thank you, it's really kind of you. Leela, please stay,' she implored.

'Come to Richard's,' said Leela, hoping Amy wouldn't.

'No, it's fine. Thank you, thank you both. Can I give you some money for the cab?'

'Don't be silly, we were going this way anyway.'

'Goodnight.' She hurried out, her bag half open, towards the door, and they watched her find the key and wrench it open.

'I hope she's going to be all right,' Richard said.

'I wanted to stay with you,' Leela said. She had spent the evening preventing herself from guarding him, and she

113

wanted to retreat into his hermetic world, where she would be unhappy but not under threat of loss.

'Maybe you should have gone with her. She seemed really upset.'

Leela was silent. Later, they discussed Amy, and she explained that her friend could be inconsistent, selfish, and on occasion untrustworthy.

15

She woke early, used to going to the gym. With the new job, the commute had become longer. When she came into consciousness, it was as though at the tail end of a dream: no, she was thinking, no, no. She became aware of the duvet, the blinds, the room, its walls, where she was. She rejected all of these, but especially the other body in the bed. She would lie there in semi-conscious fury, thinking, this can't go on, I must do something; then she would get up and begin to make her peace with the day in small repeated actions: going to the bathroom, brushing her teeth, washing and examining her face, or going to the kitchen to make coffee; opening the living-room curtains. Summer was ending, with faded, charming days of residual warmth.

At Finchley Road she crossed the platform and waited till a Metropolitan line train rumbled up. A few people got out, and she found a seat. She carried her heavy new bag, with the laptop from work.

The train drew past neat brick houses and the backs of gardens which she liked to look into; past tower blocks, roads, bridges, and later, humdrum fields, in some of which a few horses stood chewing. She had marvelled when she'd gone for the interview: the ProPage office, which described its location as west London, seemed to be in another world. These were the suburbs, a mid-sized town not much larger and uglier than the one she'd grown up in, but as a satellite of London, people here had a confidence Leela and her contemporaries would have envied.

She'd arrived at work, or nearly, and that brought its own reluctance. She walked slowly along the platform. The tarmac had deep depressions which filled with water. Leaves, curled, forked at the ends, yellow, brown, and parchment, sometimes magenta, fell into these miniature reservoirs and were displayed.

To get to the office she walked through the shopping centre, where assistants in black clothing were brusquely rear-ranging racks of dresses, jumpers, and jeans.

The office was in a high-rise shared with other profes-sional service companies – an accountancy firm, a lawyer's. In the lobby, she waited for the lift, and stared at the points of her new shoes. When the door opened on her floor, she knew, she would walk out quite fast, as though impatient for the day to begin.

'Hey there!' She looked up at the sound of comic reproach and after a pause recognised Judy, who worked in the same part of the firm.

'Oh, sorry. World of my own,' said Leela. She smiled for Judy and regretted for herself that it wasn't possible actually to live in a world of her own. What if she had indeed devised this world? Could I have done this, she wondered of the lift, the tan stockings of the girl on her left, the horrible carpet?

'And *this* is it?' the other girl enquired, her Scottish voice full of sarcasm but also a cheer that came from her youth. Or perhaps from the fact that she was crazy. Leela grinned at her, taking in the messily scraped-back hair, the drop of eye make-up on her cheek, and the tiny rip in her black jeans, worn under a jacket.

'God, I'm so hungover,' Judy complained. The lift door opened. They shambled out together onto the fifth floor.

'Could you put this on my desk? Why don't you come and lurk near the art guys?' Judy put her bag into Leela's hand and wandered away. 'Do you want a coffee?' floated back at her.

'No thanks,' Leela said quickly. Almost no one made it strong enough. She plugged in her laptop, put Judy's bag on her desk, and logged onto the system. She must check her horoscope.

Judy came back with coffee and put it down. It spilled slightly. 'Shit …' She began to use a tissue to mop it up. Mere coffee, Leela thought, could look so offputting. Her wave of revulsion reminded her of the time just before adolescence when she'd hardly been able to eat, suddenly hyper-aware of the chomping, swallowing, digesting sounds of her family around her at the table: her mother, picking up a piece of chapati and scraping after a last lick of gravy; her sister eating in enormous, swift mouthfuls; her father's small teeth quietly grinding at a piece of meat. She remembered a poem for children about a boy who becomes translucent, so that everyone can see his food as it is masticated, passes through the first part of the gut, then turns into chyme – a word that by itself could make her feel sick. And what happened at the end of the poem? Did the entire family kill themselves because life had become too disgusting? She didn't remember.

'So why haven't I seen you for a few days? You went some-where, didn't you – no, wait,' Judy was saying. She flicked the tissue into the bin. 'I remember. You went to a wedding.'

'Yeah, one of Richard's friends from school.'

'Where was it again?'

'Nowhere. Devon. Beautiful place, estuary, cottages, that sort of thing. Country church. We stayed in a really nice hotel.'

'Uh huh?' Judy was picking black nail varnish from one fingernail.

'Mm, that's very lady-like of you.'

The other girl grinned. 'It is, isn't it? So, did you have fun at the wedding?'

I hate weddings, Leela contemplated explaining, and I hate enforced fun. Richard's friends make me nervous in large groups and, sometimes, bored in small ones, and I spent the entire time before and most of the time during it waiting for him to embarrass me by flirting with someone or just make me feel crap by staring at someone. She thought tangentially of the man she'd seen at the wedding. She'd been introduced to him, but forgotten his name. He'd come on his own, seemed to know few people, and had kept to himself, inappropriately dressed in chinos and a torn jumper, looking cheerful. She'd envied him because he was alone.

But she hadn't been at ProPage long enough to start being honest. 'Yeah, it was great,' she said.

Judy gave her a bored look. 'Right,' she said. Her computer whirred into life. 'Now,' she said, 'which piss-boring page of the leading business-to-business monthly for reinsurers should I lay out first?'

'Yeah, let's go out for a quick drink.' They were at Amy's flat. 'I'm not really up for anything big though.'

'I'm *so* not up for anything big. Jeez.' Amy shut the door behind her with a bang. They ran down the narrow stairs and were in the street, then the main road.

'How about here? It's pretty average, but doesn't look horribly loud,' Amy said. And, at the bar, 'I think I'd like white wine. What about you? Shall we just get a bottle? It's less than two glasses each would be.'

Leela carried the bottle, Amy the glasses. They sat at a wooden table on an elevated platform with a railing round it: an imitation, several times removed, of something in a nineteenth-century painting.

'Cheers. So, how's it going with Andrew?'

'Oh, it's been a hideous week or two. First, I saw him three times the week before last.'

'Wasn't that nice?'

'It was *lovely*. It was lovely. But then I didn't hear from him for a week. He was in Brussels, he was doing some stuff. Then he and Laura went away for a few days. It feels so shit not to hear from him after spending so much time together.'

'It must do.' Leela tried to look sympathetic. They'd had a conversation in which Amy had berated her for not being supportive enough about Andrew. And Leela's interest in talking about him had increased since she'd met him.

Amy's voice had risen, and a couple of men at another table looked at them curiously. Leela was aware of their slight movements, and their voices lowering, then she stopped looking. Something caught the corner of her eye: one of them was waving at her and Amy. Leela, startled, peered at him, but didn't recognise him.

'I know, I know, it's my own fucking fault,' Amy was saying savagely.

'It's not easy though,' Leela said. 'I mean, what are you supposed to do? At least he's interesting and nice and intelligent. He's not threatened by you.'

'Obviously,' Amy snorted.

'I don't really get the whole thing. I don't get what's supposed to be the thing to do.'

'I should have met the man I was going to marry at university,' Amy said with irritation.

Leela grinned. 'Too late now.'

'I'm sure that's what was supposed to happen.'

The wine tasted sweet, but only faintly. Leela was hungry and drank more, till the sugar and alcohol hit her. Amy tipped the last drops into her glass.

'Another bottle?'

'Uh, well —'

When she returned to the table, Leela was declining an offer of a drink from the man who'd waved at them.

'Why won't you let us buy you ladies a drink?'

'Because,' Amy interjected, 'we already have a drink. See? Have wine. No want to talk to you.'

Fuelled by their indignation, they drank faster.

'So, what's happening? I need to know everything,' Amy said.

'I've got to go to this hideous dinner thing tomorrow. I suppose it might be all right. One of Richard's friends. He lives with his parents, in Richmond or something.'

'Why will it be hideous?'

'Because they're cripplingly posh. What am I supposed to do with my knives and forks? I mean, no, don't tell me, I know what to do with them. But what the fuck? There always ends up being some small random other knife sitting about that you didn't reckon on, and you end up buttering your bread with the *proper* knife, then have to eat your dinner with the little one and look like a cretin.'

'Supper. I've started calling it supper.'

'What?'

'I think it's more posh,' Amy articulated clearly, 'so I've started saying supper.'

'For fuck's sake.'

It turned out the second bottle was also over. Both of them were drunk, but it was only nine. Amy had a brainwave. 'I can't get another hangover. Let's go back to my flat and do an aerobics DVD.'

'What are you *talking* about?'

'It'll make us metabolise the alcohol faster. We've just poisoned ourselves. Our livers are dying.'

'Cheery.'

They went to her house, and Leela lay on the sofa, the room doing aerobics around her head, while Amy watched an apparently interminable film on television, saying that staying up would allow the alcohol to be processed. Leela fell asleep. The next day she had to rush, shower, borrow clothes, and scramble to get to work.

'Thank you,' Leela heard herself say for the fifth time in about three minutes. She couldn't remember the rules. In her family people said it all the time, even when being served in restaurants; later, she'd come to suspect the habit betrayed how middle class she was. She was irritated with herself for even thinking about it; she was what she was – wasn't she? 'Supper' popped into her mind. They had popped round for supper. She tensed and waited to hear someone say it.

'The paella is delicious,' Richard said. He smiled at Seb's mother, who smiled back at him. Leela echoed the praise.

'It's a family recipe,' Seb's mother said. 'We get the rice from a place on the King's Road, it makes all the difference. And Seb went to get the mussels this morning because the fish man didn't come this week.'

'The mussels are yummy,' Leela said.

The large room had a rustic, somewhat Spanish feeling, perplexing given that the house was in Richmond. In other circumstances, Leela might have warmed to Seb's mother. She was very English, and rather upper class – his father, who spent part of the year in Spain, was a painter. Leela hadn't heard of him. There was a studio in the house, and various canvases, some unframed, hung or were propped here and there. She liked them: they were warm abstracts that looked like aerial views of seascapes, different rich blues, greys and greens that made her think of reefs, or masses of seaweed.

Seb's mother, who had been a star showjumper, was a pro-hunting campaigner. Leela had always been against the idea of hunting, mainly on the grounds of the loathsomeness of those who seemed to do it. Was it so much worse, she now wondered, to chase and murder fox babies than to coop up chickens so they couldn't move, then eat their eggs? She winced at the thought of cows being milked by machines, compassion she couldn't justify for suffering she was unable to measure.

She caught Seb's mother giving her an odd look and realised she had stopped eating. Seb smiled and poured her more wine.

'So, Leela, have you been to Avondale yet?' This was their school, Richard's and Seb's.

'Not yet. But then Richard hasn't been to visit my comprehensive yet,' she pointed out with a grin. Richard smiled; Esme, Seb's mother, looked unamused. Everyone had a show-piece conversation about capital punishment, in which Leela took the opposite line to the one she thought she believed. These sorts of discussion were not foreign; she was comfortably back in the world she'd grown up in, where children were expected to have interesting things to say. But, when she made a distinction between the persistence of life and its quality, and which might be considered more important, she found Seb looking apologetic and his mother appalled. 'As a Christian, I'm afraid the sanctity of life is something I take very seriously,' Esme said curtly.

Leela nodded and was silent. Later, as she was eating a syllabub, she thought, but what about the mussels and prawns in the paella? She felt that it hadn't been what she'd said, but the person she was, in an undefined way: her foreignness, but disappointing lack of corresponding aristocratic or artistic background – her mother was a lawyer, her father a language teacher, not that Esme had asked – or even her gender, that meant that Esme would have preferred, somehow, that Leela be a little bit prettier, or somewhat more silent.

But all of this might have been untrue.

Seb's younger sister, whom Leela had an idea Richard had always thought pretty, wasn't there; she was at university in Bristol. Her name was India.

Richard's dad came for a visit. Richard, flushed and pleased, said they'd gone to lunch in an Indian restaurant in Mayfair. 'You'd have liked it, the food was delicious. We'll have to go some time.'

Leela didn't argue with him. She went out with Judy after work.

'Do you want to go somewhere round here, then go back into town?'

'Are you crazy?' Judy said. 'Have you seen the places round here?'

She lived south of the river, Leela north, so they went for a drink at Baker Street, then to a restaurant that served crêpes and galettes.

Judy listened, her head on one hand, as Leela explained the situation with Richard, his father, and the unusual living arrangement. 'So you don't really see him when his dad's here?'

'I do, but not that much. He calls if he's free.'

Judy's eyes narrowed. Then she smiled, and reached for the carafe. 'Let's have another drink,' she said.

Leela went home, which was now a flat share in Marylebone, in the apartment owned by a woman named Dee Dee, who had a seven-year-old daughter, Alisha. Dee Dee wore acrylic nails, and kept her Mars bars and cans of Coca-Cola in the fridge, so that vegetables had to be eased in between them. She was in theory an accommodating but in practice exasperated flatmate. She was pathologically clean, and had given Leela basic instructions when she moved in. The sink had to be washed every time dishes were washed in it; it must then be wiped with a paper towel to prevent water marks.

Dee Dee went to sleep early most days, and Leela was able to steal into the flat, walk to the kitchen and sink, get a glass of water, wipe the sink (Dee Dee would notice if she hadn't) and go to her room. She kept the door locked; Dee Dee had said she might.

When she was in bed, her phone beeped. It was a text from Richard: Goodnight sweetie xx. She replied: he called, upbeat after a nice evening with his father. He left it slightly too long to ask about her evening, and in the small lag her rage mounted. She gave herself permission to be angry.

'Why are you gloating about your evening? What's wrong with you?'

'What do you mean gloating?'

'You're always going on about things you do with your dad, but you won't let me meet him. It's deliberately cruel.'

'No it's not. I've explained –'

'I don't give a fuck about your explanation.'

It went on, increasingly vicious in words and forms, but a part of her was nonetheless aware of the moonlight, cold and quiet, moving across the room through not-quite-closed curtains.

16

She was up quickly, out of bed, then in the kitchen, putting on the kettle, but Richard was almost unbelievably slow. She put a cup of coffee near him when she came back for a towel. He rolled over and smiled at her, the secretive smile of a child who knows he is loved. She felt a kick of repulsion.

'Coffee.'

'Thanks sweetie.'

She went to the bathroom, turned on the shower, brushed her teeth, examined her face in the mirror. Her eyes narrowed. She got into the shower, soaped, washed her hair and emerged in a towel, got her coffee, heard the noises of Dee Dee waking up, a radio, and went back to her room. The light was still on, the curtain unopened. Richard was up, bumbling, looking at his hair in the mirror, then rifling through his bag.

'I don't know if you have time to take a shower, unless you hurry,' she said.

'I'll hurry.'

He took the other towel and headed to the bathroom. She dressed and put on some make-up, the eyes still severe. He came back, gave her a kiss, and she recognised and silently condemned the smell of his mouth beneath the toothpaste.

'Sorry sweetie, I'll only be a minute.'

'I'm getting late.'

'I know, I'm sorry, give me a minute.' He pulled out clean boxers and put them on, a shirt, then his perennial grey jumper and a pair of corduroys. He looked at her, suddenly appealing. 'Can I borrow some socks?'

She was exasperated. It was a bone of contention, quasi-humorous, that he took her socks and didn't return them. She fished in a drawer. 'Here.'

'Thanks sweetie.'

He sat on the bed to put them on properly, irritating her further, then checked his satchel. They could leave. She marched towards the station; he followed.

'Hey, slow down, you're leaving me behind.'

She turned. Her face was a mask of rage, but that was ordinary. Today, though, he hurried closer, shifted his satchel strap, hunched his shoulders, and took the hand she reluctantly gave him.

'I'm feeling a bit odd,' he said.

'Odd how?' She tried to pull him along faster.

'A bit tender. Like you don't really want me around.'

Near the station, a bus roared by. A shiny cab swung in front as they were about to cross the road. Leela nearly tutted. When the cab had passed they crossed, in the opposite direction to a flow of men and women in stiff, heavy overcoats. How neat their facade was, she thought.

'I'm worried about being late again. You don't get what it's like,' she bit out.

'I know. Sorry, sweetie.' It was annoying, this faux humility.

They arrived at the tube; she would go one way, he another.

'See you tonight?' he said. He looked tall; his skin was bad right now.

'I might just have a night at mine,' she said. She imagined blissful solitude.

'I can come over again,' he said quickly.

'No.' She paused. 'Okay, I'll come to yours.'

'See you later, sweetie.' He swooped in for a kiss and was gone.

Leela hurried through the turnstile.

'So things are going better?'

Leela shrugged. 'I think I just don't care as much any more.'

Judy raised an eyebrow.

'Is it lunchtime yet?' Leela asked.

The other woman grinned. 'That's the sixth time you've asked. Why did you come with me if you were going to get this bored?'

'I thought you needed one of the edit people in case you had to cut text.'

'Hypothetically, yes,' said Judy.

'To blame, in case there's a typo or a hanging sentence.'

Judy grinned. 'Now you've got the idea. Okay, we can go. I'll finish the rest after a break.'

They stood, found their coats again at the outer door, and were leaving the printer's when they nearly bumped into someone tall, dark, bearded, slightly plump, oddly familiar.

'Oh, hi!' He paused, staring at them, particularly Leela. He stuck out a hand. 'Roger Wilkes. From the wedding.'

'Oh, of course. Hi, how are you?'

He looked from one to the other of them. 'This is my friend Judy, my colleague,' Leela said.

'Roger, hi.' Judy's voice was uninflected. Leela listened neurotically for a shade of mocking.

'Um, are you going for lunch?'

'Yeah, we're going for a sandwich.'

'Oh, okay.' He hesitated.

Someone else was pushing the glass door behind Leela, who jumped aside. 'Ooh, sorry.'

'Well, maybe see you later?'

'Okay!'

They took the stairs.

'Who's that?' Judy asked.

'I met him at the wedding, remember, the one I went to in Devon? I wouldn't have remembered his name, actually. He seemed nice though. He was on his own.'

'Hm, he's sort of cute.'

'You think? Not a bit fat?' Leela stopped at the bottom of the stairs.

'I think he's attractive.'

'Yeah?'

'Yeah,' Judy said. 'I like that Mediterranean look. A bit stocky, a bit hairy.'

'Who would have guessed?'

The outer door led onto the high street and a blast of cold air and pre-Christmas sullenness. The decorations were up.

'Jesus. Look at this weather.'

Leela was tormented agreeably through lunch and the afternoon by the desire to see Roger again, and find out if he was indeed handsome, or if she was attracted to him. Either or both of these questions might be answered by another chance encounter on the stairwell.

What had he been doing in the building? She didn't think he worked there, but perhaps he too had some sort of journal to produce, or something he was getting printed.

'Do you want some coffee?' she asked Judy in the afternoon.

'Yeah. Uh – actually, no, that machine coffee makes me feel sick.'

'Shall I go to the place in the mall?'

Judy looked up, then at the clock on her screen. 'Forget it, it's three forty-five now, we won't even be here that late with any luck.'

'I might go anyway, just to get some air.'

Judy raised her eyebrows, and said nothing. Leela, unsure whether she felt excited or slightly sick, went into the stairwell, put on her coat, and descended the steps. She walked to the coffee place and ordered an Americano and a cappuccino. She returned, meditating on the way the suburban landscape was completely without beauty. There was a branch of a tree hanging over a wall near the shopping centre; a couple of leaves still clung to the knobbly wood. If her eyes had been better, if she could have looked more closely, would she have found more to see in it?

She carried the coffee upstairs and met no one.

'So January is closed?'

'Yeah. Thank fuck.'

'Right.' Leela continued to hover. 'What about *Cement Trade*?'

'Huh?' The other girl looked up, and pushed hair away from her face. 'Which one?'

'Um, March?'

'Are you feeling okay?'

Leela grinned and melted away. 'Yeah, I mean, yeah. Just – yeah.'

'Wait! You want to go to the printer, don't you? And meet Alfred Molina?'

'Who?'

'The swarthy man, Ha ha,' Judy began to cackle, though to Leela's relief softly. 'You have a *thing* for him.'

'No I don't.'

'You do!'

'I think,' Leela said, her dignity impaired only by a grin that seemed to stretch over her entire head, 'that you are forgetting I have a boyfriend.'

'Someone is.'

'Oi.'

Judy smiled, picked up her water bottle, and walked towards the passage.

For about three days and four nights Leela dwelt in a romantic-sexual haze. She had experienced this numerous times, with objects that had included boys at school, Robert Redford in *Out of Africa*, an unattractive occasional tutor at university, men on the tube. Now she dreamt of Roger, who in the daydreams had come increasingly to resemble Alfred Molina – an actor, she discovered – because she couldn't remember how Roger actually looked. He was tall, a bit paunchy, dark, and pretty hairy, she remembered that much. His hairy wrists and dark eyes now became an erotic focus. Roger – strange name – was no doubt passionately artistic. The sex was amazing. The intensity of their bond was extraordinary. She imagined a misunderstanding that briefly separated them, and led to an even more passionate reunion.

It passed the train journey, when she sat soporifically staring at misty, rain-dampened outer-city fields and miserable horses. It passed the moments when she reviewed the next quarter's editorial budget in an Excel sheet for each title. It nearly passed the horrid cups of coffee either from the Klix machine on their floor, or from the building's cafeteria on the third floor, where of a morning she went to get a drink and examine the oleaginous bacon rolls.

She mentioned it to Richard, wondering why he didn't see into her thoughts and discern the obvious interest. 'I met Roger, remember, the guy from Christian and Elisa's wedding? The one who was on his own?'

'The guy with the beard?'

'Yeah.'

'Oh, really,' Richard said. He didn't lift his head from the magazine; he continued to read, massaging his earlobe. 'Where did you meet him?'

'At the printers. We went to check on the January issues, you know, sign the pages off.'

'Oh, okay.'

'Yeah, they sometimes have last-minute changes. Judy went to look at everything again, and I went as well, partly in case they needed someone from edit, you know, to change stuff.'

'Mm?'

'Yeah, so we bumped into him there.'

'What was he doing there?' He was still reading.

'No idea,' Leela said. It bothered her. Why hadn't she found out?

'Oh yeah, now I remember. He owns that furniture business, doesn't he?'

'Does he?'

'Yeah, quirky upholstered chairs or something. He has a thing, in west London somewhere. Notting Hill, somewhere like that.'

'Oh, okay. So why the printers?'

'Catalogue?'

There was a silence. Richard broke out, with a resurgence of passion, '*Prospect* is so well edited. It's such a great magazine!'

134

Eleven o'clock. Leela got up to go to the cafeteria, came back with a cup of horrible coffee and a fruit salad that she would eat too quickly and which might give her indigestion but would fend off hunger. The kiwi would be surprisingly tasty. The pineapple would be unripe. The orange would be insufficiently peeled. The grape would be sour.

She opened the flimsy plastic box and yellow juice spurted onto her newspaper. She wiped it away, sat down, stuck the little fork into the grape and realised she had an email.

The grape turned out to be sweet.

The email's sender was Roger.

'Dear Leela,' it began, and she read other words, 'the other day', 'see you', and a mobile number. Her immediate feeling was delight, the usual mysterious intimation that the world did in fact agree to her desires, that she was as magically connected to it as she had always sensed, while sometimes fearing this was not the case; this was followed by sorrow that possessing the content of the email meant losing the promise it retained while unread.

She read the words several times.

Dear Leela,

It was very nice if unexpected to see you the other day at Quickprint and I looked for you and your friend in the evening when I was leaving but didn't see either of you. Do you ever make it to the wilds of Notting Hill or Kensington? Let me know if you do and you feel like a cup of coffee when in the area. I almost never leave the workshop/office/house but it

might be worth texting before dropping in. I'm on
07949 885324.

    Roger W.

She moved to call Judy to her desk, then remembered Judy was on leave for a couple of days. She thought. How could she get to Notting Hill? And when?

She must reply immediately, but she must also not reply immediately in order not to appear as though she had been waiting for the email.

Forgetting she already had a cup of coffee, she went to the cafeteria for another, and only the bemused, slightly irritated expression of the cashier, a wisp of dyed blonde hair escaping from her polyester cap onto her tired face, brought her back to herself.

The next morning, when leaving and putting a cup of tea into a bleary Richard's hand, she said, 'I might go for coffee with Roger some time. From the wedding.'

'Oh, did you bump into him again?'

'He has a studio in Notting Hill,' Leela said. Though this didn't answer the question, Richard nodded. 'Today?'

'Not today.'

'Okay. See you later then?'

'Sure.'

She left his house, feeling that things between them were strange, and yet satisfied with the way in which they were strange.

debt; have Roger's number; call her. When she got home she would have a sickening will write a late. Or she'd text. No, she'd texted.

A series of short, flirtatious emails with Roger resulted in an appointment to have a drink after work in Notting Hill. Leela dressed with care. She told Richard where she was going. He would be out with three school friends. Leela had been staying more in the flat in Marylebone, squeezing her existence between Dee Dee's strictures of domestic hygiene. She felt harassed and at home, and enjoyed her aloneness. She would read a bit, go out to buy food, and cook something simple: half a packet of little pasta envelopes stuffed with a sticky mixture of cheese and vegetables, and half a tub of sauce. She would wash the dishes, wash and wipe the sink, make a cup of tea and retreat to her room. Its small window and view onto more brick and backyard made her think of the backs of houses, which had always meant an entry into London, through suburbs of terraced housing: brick buildings, bare and set in gardens that held small squares of grass, flower beds, a woman sunbathing, a man listening to the radio, children, a paddling pool, a dog, a tree-like drying rack spinning in the wind.

She thought of herself as more distinct from Richard. With the absence of anger came a lack of attachment.

On the day she was supposed to meet Roger the February issue of *Construction Monthly* experienced a glitch; one or more of the files turned out to be corrupted, and she had to stay late at work. There was then a delay on the Metropolitan line, and the train sat at Harrow-on-the-Hill. She realised she didn't have Roger's number with her. When she got home she sent him a text explaining why she was late. 'Another time,' he suggested.

Richard was still out. Leela, in her lamp-lit room with thoughts of escape, freedom, irony at her own desires, and the usual subterranean pleasure at finding herself alone when she had expected to be out, daydreamed, read a magazine, ate her pasta, and felt sleepy.

Walking from the tube on a misty evening ten days later, she put a hand deeper in her coat pocket. It was cold; the night sparkled. Notting Hill Gate was different at this time, its cheerful, rackety shops shuttered, and the stream of people from the tube absent.

She held her A–Z and scanned it. A right, then a left, then a small mews – there it was on the map, its name in letters so cramped they didn't fit in the street. She began to walk. There was a large house on the first corner. Near it, a thuggish tomcat sat flexing his shoulders. When he saw her, he let out a rising cry, prrrk? He minced over, back arched, asking to be patted. She chuckled, paused, and obliged. The animal, brow furrowed, intent on his own need, purred loudly, and rubbed against her calves.

'I have to go. Be good,' she said after a minute. She patted the top of his head.

He blinked, and sat down comfortably to wait as she walked on.

The street's stucco houses were set back, with abundant hedges, wrought-iron railings, and intricately organised gardens that mimicked pastoral profusion. She imagined going up one of the paths, a well-liked visitor, and being welcomed into a lighted ground-floor room lined with bookshelves.

The mews entrance was a dark corridor leading into a back area of coach houses. Which number was it? The door above a small, fire-escape-like staircase opened, and a man emerged. The light behind him threw out his shadow, wavering, implausibly tall. He paused.

'Hello there,' said Roger quietly.

'Hi,' Leela said. 'I wasn't sure which house it was.'

He remained silhouetted for a moment. Then he said, 'Come up. I thought we'd have a drink then maybe go out.'

'Sure,' she was saying, but he'd already stepped back, and opened the door wider. She made her way up the thin iron steps. A vine covered part of the building.

'Hello,' he said again when she got to the top.

'Hi,' she said. He stepped in, and bent to kiss her lightly on each cheek. He smelled lemony. In the partitioned space inside, light shone off amenable surfaces: wood, a rug, the spines of books.

'It's nice,' Leela said.

'The workshop's downstairs. When I say workshop, it's converted from a garage.' He smiled. She smiled back. Roger walked to a wide, pale wooden kitchen counter and took out two glasses. 'White? I have some open. Or I can open a bottle of red.'

'White's great.' She watched him pour the cold, faintly green liquid into each glass.

'Cheers,' he said, extending his glass.

'Cheers.'

He was dressed in slightly nicer versions of normal clothes: navy cotton trousers, a white shirt that looked soft, a brown belt and shoes. She had an almost superstitious feeling towards his possessions.

The warm light was pleasant.

'Let's go and sit down,' he said. He walked to the living room. Leela sat on a couch with a kilim in front of it. He put on a CD. A trumpet sounded: a pop song of the moment.

'Oh, I like this song,' she said with pleasure.

'Yeah? Lucia, who works next door, keeps playing it. She gave me a copy. What sort of thing do you like listening to?'

'Oh,' Leela squirmed, 'you know, mostly, er, stuff from the sixties and seventies. I love Nick Drake. I've been listening to the Supremes. Some Motown.' Adolescent fears of being uncool led her to sound bored.

Roger looked disappointed.

'What about you?' she asked quickly.

'Oh, some seventies stuff. Some folk, some jazz. I like finding new things.'

She nodded, crossed her legs, held in her stomach, smiled. Carefully, she held the wine glass by its stem.

Roger removed a pouch of tobacco and a packet of papers from his pocket.

'Do you mind if I smoke?' he asked.

'No, of course not.'

'Are you sure?' His large eyes were hazel, she saw. 'I can smoke out of the window.'

'Don't be silly, it's your house.'

'No,' he murmured, 'it matters that you're comfortable.'

'How about if I pinch one?' Leela asked with a grin.

'You smoke?'

'Sometimes. I used to, in Paris.'

He smiled, a flash through the beard. 'Smoking in France doesn't count.'

'I know. That's what you feel, because everyone's doing it. It seems positively health-giving. Can I have a skinny one please?' she asked. His fingers were parcelling out a little bundle of the brown and yellow fibres, teasing them into a line on a cigarette paper.

'Is this skinny enough?' He held up the cigarette.

'Thanks.' She looked down at it. 'You do it so neatly. I'm no good at it.'

'You could try one of those machines,' he suggested. He rolled another. As he licked the gum, his eyes met hers.

'I guess. I didn't want to smoke so much anyway, it doesn't suit me.'

He dimpled and smiled again. 'Doesn't suit your image?'

'Oh no, not that. I love it as an image. Especially rollies.'

He held out the lighter. She put the cigarette in her lips and leant forwards, mocking herself for the self-conscious eroticism of it. The cigarette caught; she inhaled immediately, and began to cough. Roger, who had lit his and taken a sharp, long inhalation, raised his eyebrows while blowing out.

Leela laughed and coughed. 'I know, could I be any more sophisticated?'

He smiled. 'You're adorable.'

She was both thrilled and mildly miserable. She shouldn't be doing this. He smoked, then stood up.

'Let's open the window anyway, it'll be nicer.'

'Okay.'

He threw open the window, and she stood near him smoking and shivering in the night air.

He smiled.

'What?'

'I've never seen anyone smoke a cigarette with such concentration. You make it look like it's a joint.'

She grinned. 'I don't smoke that much any more.' She wished the irritating complications of having a boyfriend hadn't existed. She imagined a later stage, of freedom, and the right thing appearing. A nicotine rush lifted her on a wave of euphoria and nausea. She conscientiously smoked the cigarette till its end.

Roger took large, silent inhalations. When he'd finished he put out the cigarette, picked up the ashtray and took it with him to the kitchen. His glass was empty, and he came back with the bottle.

'Shall we put this out of its misery?'

'Okay,' Leela said. She felt slightly sick, and a little drunk.

He poured more of the cold, metallic wine into her glass, and the rest into his. They stayed at the window.

'I like it here at night. The yard's busiest in the day. I have the workshop, and there are other workshops here. One guy who lives here, in the biggest flat, is a banker. See there?' He made Leela lean half out of the window, and took her elbow to push her further, till she could see the corner house, which extended over the cobbled pathway.

'So he's not at home during the day.' She put her foot back on solid ground and leaned against the sill again. Roger smiled.

'He's not home. Then there's Derek, he's a cabinetmaker, he's opposite me. And in the middle, Lucia. She makes clothes, really cool stuff, and reconditions vintage dresses.'

'Oh, cool.'

'Yeah. She is very cool. You see these amazing women coming to her door,' he said, and smiled. 'Models, women with rich husbands. Amazingly dressed. High heels, great clothes.'

'Right.' She was slightly put out, and revised her earlier guilt about Richard.

He closed the window. 'Shall we go and get a bite?'

'Sounds great.'

'I'm starving,' Roger said.

17

'I can't believe it,' said Richard. He clutched his hair. 'I thought things were going better?'

Leela tried to be attentive. She sat in the chair and watched him pace around. Earlier, she thought, I would have cared that he was upset. I would have worried about whether he loved me.

What was the relationship between these two states, each of which could be filed under her name as behaviour that belonged to her?

'I'm sorry,' she said. 'I think things just went on like that for too long. It's not anyone's fault or anything.'

She began to wonder how long this would have to continue. It was darkening outside; Saturday afternoon, miserable buses threaded their way north from the West End.

He came to sit near her; he began to pull a more assertive manner about him. 'You'll have to give me time,' he said. 'It's not going to be easy, getting over this.' He was planning, organising, not regretting. 'What about if I said we could think about living together after a year or two? And decide then?'

She looked at him, slightly incredulous. 'There's no point,' she said. 'Aren't we both sick of this?'

A few days later, a moment when he stood in front of his wardrobe, taking off his shirt. 'You're going to do it again,' he said.

'Do what?'

'Find someone else who's in awe of you and then dump them.'

'Who's in awe of me?'

'Everyone. All your friends look up to you,' he said.

She sat on the bed staring at him. He'd asked her to stay the night. She'd agreed to spend time with him as he wanted, during the process of their separation, though the promise gave her a tug of dread. Still, it would have been too unkind, wouldn't it, not to do what another, especially someone so close, wanted in this situation?

They lay in the darkness, and she began to fall asleep, still aware of her silence and rigidity.

In the middle of the night, he said, 'Is there someone else?'

'What?'

'Is there someone else?'

She was lulled by the hours of dispassionate, almost comradely conversation. 'No,' she said.

'Oh. Because I told my dad, and that's what he asked.'

She considered. 'Nothing happened, but I realised that I was attracted to Roger, that time I went out with him, and that made me feel things were over with us.'

He, ordinarily so languid, moved in a whirlwind of duvet and anger, and was standing. 'I knew it. You complete whore!'

'What?' But he wasn't pretending to be angry. He picked up the bedside lamp and threw it against the cupboard. 'Just fuck off. Bitch!'

'But I didn't do anything. Why did you ask if you didn't want to know?'

'Get out!'

She was already near the door, her bag and clothes in her hands, dressing. She quickly put on her underwear and a sweater, picked up her bag, skirt and shoes, and ran out of the door. On the landing, in the clean, lit corridor of the mansion flats, with its blush carpet and waxed woodwork, she stopped to put on her skirt and shoes, wondering if a businessman with a small suitcase or an elderly woman would pass on the stairs, and look reprovingly at her.

In the street she stood irresolute. It was dark and cold; her phone said 03:20. She called a cab firm: it would take half an hour. 'I'm on my own,' she told the man in the office, 'please send it as soon as you can.' She felt pity for herself, as an abstract proposition, a woman alone in the middle of the night in a deserted part of the city. She saw a black cab and ran to wave it down. The driver stopped; Leela opened the door, and gave her address.

When she was in her room, shivering back to warmth, she sent an email to her parents, telling them briefly what had happened, and a longer one to her sister. She'd call Neeti the next day. She changed the password for her email account, unplugged the telephone, and turned off her mobile. She woke at midday to knocking on the door. Dee Dee ushered in Richard. He looked haggard.

'Where have you been?' he said. 'I haven't slept.'

Leela looked at him and her landlady, who disappeared down the corridor rather slowly, still smoking.

She closed the door of her room behind Richard. He had not showered, she thought; or he smelled of himself more strongly than usual. He wore jeans and a t-shirt, and his woollen jacket.

'I was worried, I tried to call you,' he said.

'Isn't that a bit post-fact? You threw me out in the middle of the night.'

He looked briefly embarrassed. 'I was very angry,' he said.

'Why are you here?'

'Look, you can leave your things in my place for as long as you need to,' he said. He seemed to have made a list of things to say. He half sat, half leaned against the edge of her MDF pine-finish desk. 'I know it won't be easy for you to move them, it's not even that big,' he peered around, 'in here.' He stopped. 'Are you going tell people what you've done?'

'How do you mean?' She sat on the bed cross-legged.

'With Roger.'

'I didn't do anything with Roger. I didn't even hold his hand. I made it clear we were together.'

'But you will now, won't you?'

The usual instinct to please was quiet. 'That's my business.'

'Don't, Leela,' he said suddenly. 'Don't for a while. Three months, six months. Don't go out with him.'

'You can't keep telling me what to do. I said I wanted to break up two weeks ago.' The muscles in her legs grew tense with the absurdity of it.

He seemed to relax. 'I'm meeting Johnny for lunch,' he said for no reason. 'Sushi. It should be nice.' They had discussed, the previous night, before the conflagration, how he might move forward, see his friends, and rebuild a sense of his life independently from her.

'Are you.' But why was he telling her this now?

He nodded. Abruptly, he said, 'It hurts, you know. It really hurts.'

'You threw me out at three in the morning, and the only reason I was there was because you asked me to be.'

He got up. 'I thought I'd buy a new mattress,' he said. 'Make a new start.'

'Okay.' She sat, uncomfortable in her pyjamas; he felt like a stranger.

'I found a place … Mattresses turn out to be pretty fucking expensive.'

She nodded.

'Do you want to come for a coffee with me? For an hour? I've got to kill some time before lunch. Johnny can't make it till two.'

Leela blinked. She said quietly, 'No. No I don't.' Ought it to have made her triumphant, or angry, this ridiculous situation? I have longed for this indifference, she thought, and not found it, and now I have it but without enjoyment or sadness either.

'Okay.'

She stood, and reluctantly he began to move towards the door of her room. She opened it, and walked to the front door. An intrigued Dee Dee looked out from the kitchen.

Leela opened the door.

'Well, bye,' Richard said. 'It feels strange not to call you sweetie, or dear,' he added.

Leela pushed the door a little wider, and he went through it.

He paused just outside. 'Are you sure about coffee?'

'Yes. Thanks.'

She shut the door on his retreating back, and walked past Dee Dee.

18

'He threw you out in the middle of the night? What a gent!' Alan began to laugh. At his familiar giggle, Leela started laughing too. It was in fact quite funny.

'He said I should stick around until he could slowly push me away. So he wouldn't feel bad about being rejected. Then I went out with someone else for a few weeks, but he dumped me.'

Alan roared with laughter. 'That's genius! Well, you have to have a rebound thing. It's the rule.' He laughed more. Leela looked at him with some disbelief, but then she chuckled too. They would reappear, these people, through the years, unexpectedly and infrequently, and sometimes they would be comforting. Especially the boys you had never been attracted to, and who had never been attracted to you, but who accepted you as a familiar part of their earlier life.

She glanced at Alan, whom she hadn't seen for a few years. What would he be like as he grew older, with a wife, children? Would he remain so laughing and pleasant, so simple? There were the other familiar but strange faces around the table, and near the bar in a knot. Amy was there. Leela saw a flash of her red hair, and heard her laugh; she was telling a story in the middle of a small circle.

A packet of crisps lay open on the table: it had been torn along one side and opened out. Just a few morsels of crisp remained, and shiny tracks of fingers on the foil.

The second time she sent her email of resignation it was accepted. She was told to leave by the end of the week. She called some of the temping agencies she had earlier worked for. She went to reregister, at Fenchurch Street, at South Molton Street, at Berners Street. She typed sample texts, and got eighty per cent accuracy, seventy per cent speed.

There wasn't much work going, the agency representatives said. They looked her over. Pencil skirt, white shirt, high heels. 'You must wear heels,' Amy had hissed, in an exasperated moment of drunken candour. 'Otherwise people won't take you seriously.'

'How long are you available for?' asked Estelle at South Molton Street.

'Six months at least, though I'm looking for a permanent post, obviously,' said Leela firmly. This, she knew from experience, was the optimum lie. Less than six months was too little for the rep to make much commission; wanting to temp forever marked you out as feckless. 'It gets harder to get a temping job when you're over thirty,' she remembered a woman at the reinsurer's office telling her, as though these typing and filing posts, paid hourly without sick leave, were exceptionally desirable.

The morning after Leela had reregistered in South Molton Street and Estelle had pursed her lips and said, 'There's so little right now – but are you available for the odd day if someone's off sick?' and Leela, again mendaciously, had said, 'Oh totally, of course, just call', her mobile buzzed at 8:14.

It was cold and dark. She had her head under the duvet, where she preferred to keep it these days. It best allowed her to smell her own fetor, to keep her eyes closed, to cry and scream silently into the padding, to pretend that the disappointing world did not exist.

Now the phone was ringing.

She lifted her head. To be sure, it was cleaner outside the duvet. It was colder too, and she heard a medium-weight rain falling with dreary regularity in the backyard.

She remembered her promise of willingness to Estelle and wanted to laugh.

'Hello?'

'Leela?' Estelle's voice was sharp. The phone had been ringing nearly long enough to go to voicemail; she would have had to call other people if Leela hadn't picked up.

'Speaking,' said Leela brightly.

The job was in Notting Hill, quite near Roger's flat. For the next three weeks she trailed there, waiting to be humiliated when she bumped into him. She replayed the moment when he'd turned to her gravely and said, 'I know this is going to hurt you but I have to say it. I don't want a relationship.'

'I know,' she had said quickly, but he'd prolonged the conversation anyway. She hadn't cried then, and he'd stopped her near his door to give her a lingering, unwanted hug, after which he'd pulled back and appraised her with his large, hazel eyes. 'You don't seem that upset,' he'd noted.

After three weeks, Leela called in sick, filed her time sheet, and on Sunday sent Estelle an email saying that her grandmother – she had none left, but felt a warm, sentimental pang for herself as she typed it – had been taken ill. She had to go to India.

BOMBAY

BOMBAY

19

'Ah, you're up,' her father said. She stood in front of him, blinking and yawning. He was sitting in one of the cane chairs; his face broke into a smile. 'Ma's gone to get a few things, she has someone coming over, but not for a while. Have some coffee? Do you want me to make you juice?'

'I'm okay,' Leela said. She wanted juice. She waited. 'I can make it,' she said.

'I'll make it for you.' He went to the fridge and removed three large smooth citrus fruit.

'Oh, mosambi?'

'Yes, these are good ones.'

'Is it the season?' she asked.

Her father sliced each mosambi in half. He took out the juicer, reassembled it, and plugged it in. She watched his hands, small and long-fingered, as they pushed each halved fruit on the rotating press. The motor hummed. Outside a bird sang. In loose cotton pyjamas, she was warm, even mildly perspiring. She became aware of the back of her neck, warm and at peace.

She sat eating quietly, cross-legged on one of the dining-table chairs. To her left, the balcony door was open, a curtain waving in the space.

The newspaper was full of unfamiliar usages – encroachment (meaning an illegal building), gift (as a verb), incidentally (meaning importantly), hutment. In the colour supplement were bad photos of people who appeared to be famous. Some looked plump; they were dressed in spangles, at parties; after that came a horoscope, the TV section, and the classifieds. She read them: rooms in South Mumbai, Rs 4,000 onwards! Call centre interviews. OPEN INTERVIEW.

'It doesn't seem that difficult to get a job,' she said.

Her father looked disparaging. 'Depends on the type of job you want. And have you any idea how many people would go for one of those things?'

'Right.' She closed the paper, looked at her coffee mug and considered whether to make more coffee.

'Have you put your geyser on?'

'Yeah.'

'It might be a good idea to have a bath now,' her father said. 'The power often goes around one o'clock.'

Leela went and washed her plate and mug and shambled past him. She passed the front door which opened. Her mother had returned.

'Ah, you're up?' she said. 'Not that it matters, but Priya and Elizabeth are coming over for coffee later. I'm just telling you.'

Leela went back to her room and shut the door as an initial precaution. She lay on the bed.

At the end of the afternoon, she set out for a walk up their quiet lane, with trees all around, and the sounds of birds. Vehicles came at her from three directions as she crossed the main road; behind, a motorbike turned in, a man called out, and in front were cars, and a bicycle coming the wrong way.

She stepped onto the high pavement. Under some trees, a fat woman in a nine-yard sari sat behind a cigarette stall. Leela picked her way past. Then the lone but busy mochi, mending someone's sandal as he smoked; she had to get off the pavement because of the knot of people near the tea stall. Thin men, who looked at her, and she strode past trying to appear indigenous, and au fait.

20

In the hut, she woke, thought about sleeping again, remembered that she had planned to rise early to swim in the sea, which was so conveniently close. When she'd arrived the previous night, she had looked at the path, heard the boom of the breakers, and gone to bed with the usual sense of excitement. Now she just felt nervous. The mild depression of the habitual oversleeper took hold; everything anticipated was already anticlimactic. She let go of the vision of herself rising with the dawn, drawn to the beach like an amphibian, swimming in the waves and then walking back up the cliff for breakfast in the café. 'I love swimming in the sea,' she heard herself say, explanatorily, to herself about herself, ruining the moment. She sighed. There had been mosquitoes in the night, not many, but lying still and waiting for them to be sated had not worked. She got up, needing to pee. The room was plain, a cement floor and a small ceiling fan. I am paying, she thought, to rent a hut similar to the one the bai at home lives in. Though with more privacy, and near the sea. The frivolity of her project was embarrassing. But she would go through with it. Afterwards, she would be able to say, 'I went travelling – in India?'

She dressed, came out of the hut, and locked the door. The world appeared, bright blue, yellow, and green. Coconut palms, and long fallen fronds on the sand; a man in a hoisted-up lungi washing under a tree; a clothes line; a bird shouting; a couple of crows on the ground fighting over a piece of coconut shell.

'Ah, morning.' It was Johnny, the man who'd rented her the room. 'You sleep late.'

'Well, I –'

He grinned and rounded the corner carrying his watering can.

When she got to the café she decided to eat breakfast and wait till the afternoon to swim.

The water was cooler than she'd imagined. She walked in, enjoying its fizz against her calves. To her right, some blond children played. They dove under enormous breakers and resurfaced neatly. The waves were bigger than she remembered, but this was still the Arabian Sea, just further down the coast from Bombay. She began to stride out. She'd forgotten the weight of the water, or the largeness and interconnectedness of the sea. A wave rose, a fat swell, and she jumped, slightly late, but it passed, setting her down. She giggled, looked down, realised another was rising next to her. She jumped as it broke, and was sucked into it, swirled around – drowning, was this what it was like? Such a busy experience, inhaling salt and water, and thrashing about?

A moment later, she was dumped on the beach. She knelt, sputtered, and hacked, then realised she was in only two or three inches of water. The blond children, aged perhaps five or six, who had been diving under the waves, were looking at her.

At lunch in the café, she eavesdropped on the next table. One of the two men, this one without much hair, tanned and in a singlet and cropped combat trousers, was talking about his job.

'I was in England, southern England,' he explained carefully. 'A place called Slough. It was soul-destroying – consumer publishing –'

Leela's head whipped round.

'Yeah, yeah,' said the toned, overtanned blonde woman in the group.

'What do you do, Jane?' asked the other man, who was mousier and European.

Jane gave Leela a slightly reproving look. 'MTV, I work in MTV. Well, no, it's – well, yes, it is pretty glam at times, but it's just work really. You know?'

'Yeah, yeah, of course,' the first man said. He stared at Jane. Leela began to evolve a fantasy in which they smiled and waved her over, and Jane realised that Leela was the coolest person there. They would go to the beach together, hang out, and the unattractive man and the less unattractive man would pay attention to Leela in the same compelled, creepy way.

Jane caught Leela's eye and looked put off. She turned, flicked her hair, and lowered her voice as she continued to talk. Leela eyed her yoga mat, rolled up with a useful little handle, and thought of the signs further along the cliff for yoga classes, and free DVD screenings. *Kill Bill*, which she'd seen, was this week's film. She imagined going to the screening and, afterwards, making friends … it went hazy. She paid the bill and went back towards her hut.

Some days later, she'd finished the book she'd borrowed from the clifftop library, which was stocked with thrillers and odd volumes left behind by previous tourists. She thought of leaving. She still hadn't been to the nearby village. There was a temple there, but a cousin had warned that, here in the south, many temples had a dress code: women must be in saris, men in a mundu. She dreaded being caught out by not knowing what to do: wave an agarbatti? Pray, certainly, perhaps offer flowers, but beyond that she had little idea.

There was a bakery café somewhere on the way to the village. She read about it in the guide book: the café, and the walk, were rehearsed so many times in her mind that the idea of either became exhausting.

'We're going to see elephants tomorrow. Have you been?' Mike said. He was a tall, sweet-faced boy, who looked both younger and older than he may have been. His brow was large and rounded, like an illustration of a child in a children's book. She had seen him in the café, looking at her and, sometimes, smiling. He sat with two older people. They looked as though they might have been his parents, but who came on holiday with their parents?

When she smiled back and said 'Hi' one day, he nearly fell off his seat. He scrambled up. 'Hi, I'm Mike.'

'I'm Leela.'

'Do you – do you want a coffee?'

'What about your friends?' The older couple had risen and were walking away.

He grinned. 'They're my parents. I think they're going to take a nap.'

'Oh.' Leela also grinned.

'My mum's just had cancer,' he said as she sat down, 'but she's in remission, so I said I'd take them away, to get over things. Get some sun.' He waved at the waiter. 'Can we have two coffees please?'

'Oh.' Leela looked down. The waiter brought them milk coffees. He stirred sugar into his. 'What do you do?' she asked.

'I make furniture.' He smiled half apologetically.

'Like a cabinetmaker?' She realised that she knew almost no one who wasn't a white-collar worker.

'Yeah. It's all right. It's a trade. Lots of heavy lifting.' He told her about people for whom he'd made cupboards, which he'd then carried up flights of stairs. 'You'd think I'd be musclier.' He indicated his lankiness. 'What about you? What do you do?' His voice was uncertain; he looked at her intently, his eyes tender, avid, doubtful.

The waiters, who'd seen her alone and him with his parents, watched them with interest, for which she suffered; but it vindicated her. She would do what she wanted, she decided. As soon as she knew what that was.

She told him about her jobs. They talked about London, about Ilford, where he lived, and his plans for his business. He had taught English in China, and enjoyed it. Then he'd started working for a man who made furniture. 'It's good money.' He'd done a City and Guilds. 'Evening class,' he sniffed, wrinkling his face.

'Did you like it?'

He smiled. 'It's pretty simple. You're not making art objects. But it's good to work with your hands.'

'Do you ever wish you'd been to university? I mean, if you enjoyed teaching and stuff?'

He shrugged, and smiled. 'I didn't want to. I wanted to work as soon as I could. And it wouldn't have been that simple. I don't know. I don't regret it.'

She nodded.

The breeze made a sigh in the palm trees above them. The sun was dimming.

He asked her if she'd have dinner with him, after he had a drink with his parents.

'Won't they mind?'

He made a conciliating grimace. 'They'll be fine. I'll go for a drink with them, then I'm free. Eight o'clock?'

At night the hotel garden became more mysterious. In clouds around the sulphur-yellow lights, insects murmured. The darkness was faintly electric. She jumped when the three noisy German boys from the next room turned the corner.

Mike was outside the café, wearing the same clothes as earlier. He was half bowed, his back to her. When she got closer she touched his elbow.

'Hi!' He jumped, then smiled, and she saw again the child-ish-old-man crinkling of his face, which he then ironed into goodwill, the entire movement swift and automatic.

He made a gesture of putting his arm around her without touching her. 'Shall we go and eat?'

'Where do you want to go?'

'One of those places along the beach? There are lots.'

'Okay.'

They walked past upturned fishing boats. 'I haven't been on this side of the beach,' Leela said.

'Oh, haven't you?' He turned to her quickly. 'I came down here to watch them bringing in the catch yesterday evening, and early in the morning once. It was amazing.'

'Was it?' She smiled. Did the foreigners who came here see more than she did, she kept wondering. They opened their eyes; she was always trying to fit things into a pattern, and not be surprised.

'They waved at me, they were really friendly,' Mike said.

She imagined herself watching the fishermen, and knew her presence would have altered the scene; they would have looked at her differently than at the foreign man.

There were four shack restaurants.

'How about this one?' he asked.

'Sure,' she said.

'Is that okay?'

'They all look the same.' Each shack had plastic tables and chairs in the sand, a smaller covered section, and menus written in coloured chalk on blackboards.

'Hello,' Mike said to the man who came forward smiling.

He'd been here for a beer, he said; he hadn't eaten. He ordered a beer and she a fresh lime soda. They discussed which fish was fresh; Leela silently worried about the cost.

Mike poured out his Kingfisher and drank from it contentedly. He rested the glass on the paper tablecloth. He was on holiday, she thought with envy. So was she, but she kept feeling she must come up with a better pretext.

'Are you looking forward to the elephants?' she asked.

He laughed. 'To be honest, it's just great to get away, get some warm weather. My parents –' his face took on a serious, protective expression when he spoke of them '– have been through a horrible time. Really horrible. Chemotherapy –'

'That makes you feel crap, doesn't it?' she asked. His anxiety made her anxious.

He waved his hand. 'It's horrible. But it's over. My mum's better. At least for now. It's good to enjoy something. And it's their anniversary.'

'How long have they been married?'

'Thirty years. They got married young. Had me. That was it.' He hesitated. 'Are you seeing anyone?'

'No. I just split up with someone. Are you?'

He hesitated again. She wondered at her own surprise.

'I have been seeing someone for a bit. Not that long. I – I think I'm onto a good thing, though.' He looked at her, and his face went through a conflict: question, avidity, then its extinguishing.

'Oh, that's great. What's her name?' She was no longer surprised.

'Sarah,' he said reluctantly.

'What does she do?'

'She works in a school.'

'Oh, nice. Does she live near you?'

He paused, and waved a hand. 'It hasn't been that long. But I think – I think I'm onto a good thing.' He sounded dogged, as though arguing with himself.

Leela nodded to show consent. The food arrived: kingfish cooked with butter and lemon, and chips on the side. The fish was very good.

'This is how I like it – simple,' Mike said. Leela, who had inwardly rolled her eyes at the thought of no chilli or anything, ate and agreed it was good.

'Are you sure you don't want a beer?'

'No, thanks.' To save money and out of an exaggerated sense of responsibility to herself, travelling alone, she didn't drink during the trip.

'Do you want another of those?' He pointed at her lime soda. She smiled and shook her head.

'So tell me about you,' he said, his eyes quick.

'Well, I was seeing someone, I was with someone for about three and a half years. In London. But I split up with him, then I was seeing someone else for a bit, now I'm single.' She fiddled with her napkin.

He watched her, eyes unquiet. 'What happened with the – with your boyfriend?'

She exhaled. 'It just went on too long. Maybe we weren't suited. Or maybe that's just what people say when they split up.'

He nodded. 'So you stopped fancying him?'

'Not that, even. He wouldn't commit, and I got really angry about it until finally I couldn't get angry any more.' She shrugged.

Mike nodded, attentive. 'And then what happened?' His long fingers plied his knife and fork.

'Then I met someone else.'

'Oh.'

Leela stopped eating so that she could better talk. 'Not like that. I didn't do anything till I'd split up with Richard. It just made me realise – if I'd still been in love with him, or believed things could work out I would never have liked someone else. When I did, I realised that was it. It'd been dragging on for too long. He couldn't make up his mind. Basically I thought, it's not that hard to know if you want to commit to someone. You pretty much know immediately, as far as I can tell.' Absent-mindedly, she ate a chip that had gone cold. Behind them, the sea did quiet, night-time things; the tide was going out.

'What happened with the other guy?'

She shrugged. 'He was a bit older. I don't know, I just didn't really get it. Then afterwards I felt stupid. He kind of made me feel stupid. When you're ten years older, you just know more stuff about life. I didn't get that, but now I do. I wouldn't let it happen again, I'd be more in control,' she said. She clutched at her empty lemonade glass. 'I'd never just go along with stuff. I've got it now. It's like you're always learning things, but never the things you need to know to stop making the same mistake in a new way.'

'It sounds like you've done a lot of thinking,' Mike said.

She felt ashamed; she had begun to tell the story in a deliberate way, but lost awareness. It had pulled her along, and she had begun to shed details, accumulate speed like a cartoon snowball.

She shrugged. 'I dunno.'

'We must keep in touch,' he said. 'I don't want this to be one of those things where you meet someone really great on holiday and have a chat and that's it.'

'Okay.'

'I mean it,' he said. 'Let me give you my number. Give me a call when you get back.'

She took out her black-backed notebook and her pen, and he took both from her. She disliked other people writing in her notebook, but watched as he wrote down his name, Mike Gibbons, and his telephone number.

'Give me your address as well,' she said. 'I could write to you.'

'I'm not very good at letters.' He wrote it down anyway. 'Call me when you're back,' he said. 'The house number's the best. Leave a message if I'm not there, and I'll call you back for sure.'

He wanted to pay for dinner, but she refused; when they said goodnight, he gave her a hug. After the elephant trip the next day, he and his parents were leaving for a bird sanctuary in the hills. Leela said she would move on in a day or two; she didn't know.

The hug had made her more lonely. The next day, eating her dosa, reading, going to the beach, she was alone in a new way. She sat on the sand, drawing in her sketchbook, and an old woman who was passing stopped to look, then tried to teach her the Malayalam word for 'cow', indicating the cow Leela was sketching to make her point.

21

'Ah, you went travelling? Where all?'

'Round the coast, Varkala, Kanyakumari, Madurai. I had the best coffee there, on the street. You know the way they pour it.' She mimed the gesture of two vessels, a yard apart.

The other girl, Chitra, smiled. She was tall and fair, with a soft face. They continued to sit in the dining room, at a corner table under the fluorescent tube lights.

Leela was divided between the pressure to be entertaining and the pleasure of a moment in which someone was listening; this was her first prolonged conversation in the hostel. 'Lots of temple towns,' she went on.

'I've been to Kanchipuram and Chidambaram,' Chitra said.

No one else was left in the room. Leela moved congealed daal around her plate. Half a leathery chapati also remained.

'I didn't go to either,' she said. 'But I did go to Rameswaram.'

'Ooh! Was it beautiful?'

'Really beautiful. The sea was incredibly blue, and calm. It made me nervous. I went on a boat trip, with this family from Indore. The boat guy said the sea is always like that at that time of year. He said in June it's flat, like glass.'

'Wow,' Chitra said. She smiled, and gathered her pots of ghee and pickle, condiments every hostel girl seemed to own.

'I went to Dhanushkodi as well. They say you can see Lanka on a clear day – but I didn't.' Her mind became blank and wondering as that day, stepping out of a rickshaw to go down to the beach. The ocean had boomed, dark blue. There had been huge breakers, and what looked like a steep shelf. She had sat on the beach for a while in her swimming costume, and a t-shirt; fishermen had pulled in their boats and thrown out ropes so that their wives could draw in the nets. The men had looked at her and the women had narrowed their eyes, telegraphing that when she began to drown, they wouldn't save her.

After some thought she had put on her trousers again. 'I didn't swim,' she told the baffled rickshaw driver.

At the end of the land was a salty promontory, fish bones and quartz, a few boats and coir huts. You looked out into space, wind, and ocean.

Chitra got up and went to the fridge to put away her stuff. Each of her bottles was labelled with her name, as per regulations. Leela followed her, already depressed by the moment when they would part for the evening. There were firm unspoken rules about new girls, who were ignored for exactly as long as making friends mattered to them. There was one girl who'd smiled at Leela and introduced herself when she moved into the corridor. But they had never spoken at length, merely exchanged 'How's it going?' and smiles en route to the communal bathroom, each clutching her plastic bucket.

She and Chitra headed into the foyer.

'Late finishing today,' remarked Mrs Pawar, one of the hostel wardens. She sat at the desk, self-consciously upright in her bright pink sari and matching, daringly low-backed blouse. Sometimes she even wore sleeveless blouses. She had recently bobbed her hair. It was an improbable crow-black.

Chitra dimpled at her. 'You know what it's like, ma'am. We were talking.' She drifted over to the pigeonholes to check her mail. Leela headed to the lift. The requirement to address the wardens as 'ma'am' so horrified her that she avoided talking to them.

'Leela Ghosh!' Pawar liked to apostrophise using the full name.

Leela turned.

'Come here.'

Leela approached. She showed her teeth. Pawar took on a reproachful look. She was a kind woman, though she would nag.

'Lee-la,' said Pawar, at length and querulously.

'Yes?'

'"Yes ma'am"', explained Pawar.

Leela remained silent.

'Your room is very untidy.'

'Where?' said Leela. She had almost no things with her – she had moved in with a suitcase. Her possessions were in the steel cupboard, or on the small shelf. Moreover, she made her bed every day.

'Your room was inspected by the committee today. Your table is very untidy.'

'Two books and a piece of paper?'

'Neat your table. And please,' said Pawar with finality and some distaste, 'try to be sincere.'

Leela gawped and moved towards the lift, which had just arrived. Chitra held open the doors, then closed the outer, then inner door. The lift stopped playing a piercing rendition of the 'Für Elise', and jerked upwards.

'"Be sincere?"' said Leela.

Chitra giggled. 'Don't worry about it. It's one of her things. "Be sincere."'

'She said my room is untidy because there are a couple of books on the desk. What the fuck?'

Chitra nodded. 'They get anal about things. It's a power trip.'

'And why was the committee in my room?'

The other girl shrugged. They had arrived at their floor. 'Don't take it all so seriously.'

'See you,' said Leela, sad that Chitra hadn't invited her to her room to chat. She moved down the corridor, and let herself into room 703. Her cell was clean and peaceful. She turned on the light and fan, shut the door, listened to the sounds of the corridor – other girls talking – and stretched out on the bed. The small fan turned crankily. The window was open onto the balcony, and the sea breeze came in clear. You could stand there in the daytime, or sit on the slightly dirty tiles, and watch a few inches of ocean shimmer not far away; the view belonged to the millionaires of Cuffe Parade, but the hostel girls had somehow appropriated it.

In the morning she lay blank after waking. The breeze came in, wilful, then went. It was too hot. A patch of sun lay across the floor: the curtains she'd bought a week earlier were slightly too short.

How did I get here? Small matters arose more urgently. The fan, turning fast in the early morning voltage, made her shiver. She pulled the sheet around her. The corridor was quiet. This would be a good time to bathe, before the bathroom became busy.

Crows quarrelled on the balcony, harsh and repetitive. She laughed, got up, went outside. The sun was already hot, almost wet in its intensity. 'Shut up!'

Two large crows, one a little younger than the other, looked round. They made clockwork noises of reproof and moved further away.

She sat cross-legged and looked down. To her left, the gardens with their large trees, then the sea, then Cuffe Parade's high-rises sparkling in the sun. On the right, the road spread out like a diagram. Buses from the depot swung out of the gate, illustrating how to manoeuvre a parallelogram around a corner.

She closed her eyes. Through the lids, orange.

For a moment there was contentment. Then she thought of a similar moment, in Roger's flat. He had without remark left a cup of coffee on the bedside table next to her, then gone to take a shower. She had half sat in bed, drinking the coffee, her mind nearly empty. From the bathroom she had heard water, Roger's beard trimmer, a snatch of song. She had been liberated in that instant from the world: she might have been said to be taking part in it, yet there was enough room for her to stand back. She hadn't considered whether she was happy, and she had been.

Revisiting the moment didn't bring the same peace. She twitched, thought of Roger – perhaps she should write to him? – and cringed, for he was bound up with her ego and meant pain and humiliation. When she dreamed of him, he appeared with a cruel face.

Inside she convulsed away from the thought. No, I'm strong and capable of … whatever. The tiles were rough under her. Would she miss breakfast, and her cup of weak coffee? That would be annoying – but there was time – but she must get to the bathroom before it became busy. She moved. Her ankle hurt against the floor. And Roger and the … but she would meet someone; something would happen. She was without faith but debilitated by hope.

She would focus on her breathing. In, the lungs were tight, then a pause; then out, slowly, the relief of having breath giving way to the urge to be rid of it. A moment's quiet, then thought started again. She sighed and opened her eyes. Below, another bus pulled into the lane. She scrambled up for her bucket, soap, and towel.

When she went to work, sitting on the top deck of the number 124 towards Worli Aagar, it would strike her, surprising her, that she was somewhere she knew – Colaba, where her aunt and uncle had lived, and the familiar road, on which many of the shops still looked the same. When she saw them, she felt she had known them even during the time she'd forgotten their existence, and the earlier life that had taken place in this small world. She remembered the thwack of thin branches on the bus's upper windows as it trundled down the Causeway past the market and the docks.

As she looked out of the window, her mind, which was always chattering underneath whatever happened, said something about the mornings, and the trip to work, and was shocked. It expected west London, rushing to the tube, privet hedges, red-brick walls, the Metropolitan line, the quiet misery of sodden concrete. She looked out instead on sunshine, banyan trees, and the Causeway, and wondered.

22

'Ah, you're here? No,' Sathya raised his eyebrows, 'that crazy bitch was asking. Between you and me, she's a bit of a stickler for timekeeping.' He threw his head back and laughed. His voice was deep and musical, but also slightly hysterical. 'Silly cow,' he said. 'Don't worry about her. I told her you were in the bathroom. Cigarette? I'm going to the gulag for one.'

Leela grinned. 'Maybe a bit early for me. Give me half an hour.'

'Not a problem. If that cretin comes with the coffee, could you grab me one? Assuming he's bothered to put any coffee in it today.'

Leela nodded. She hung her bag on her chair and turned on her computer. The processor began to whirr and gurgle; the screen thrummed into life.

Tipu Sultan, the tea boy, came in. He was shortly followed by Joan, the third person who sat in the office, which was a room in the solid mock-Gothic building.

'Ah! Leela!' said Joan. 'I was looking for you. Sathya said you'd –' The pause was dramatic and indicated doubt.

'Yes,' said Leela. She picked up papers from her desk, and moved them in front of her. They included the ten grant applications remaining from yesterday, which had to be logged in the new database, and some post addressed to her predecessor, who'd gone to England to work in an auction house. Every time Leela saw her name, Radha Gupta, on an envelope, she felt a frisson of connection, and nostalgic envy.

'Right, well, there are a lot of things piling up. I think perhaps you and I should have a meeting,' Joan said.

She had already done this three times in the fortnight Leela had been there. Each time she made Leela sit on a rickety, uncomfortable stool near her desk. Joan had the air conditioner near her turned up high. Leela sympathised in principle, but the cold made her soporific. 'Hot flushes. Think about it, explains why she's so fucking crazy,' Sathya had said over a shared Gold Flake in the gulag a couple of days earlier.

'Could I clear my pending workload first?' Leela asked. 'I don't want to let things pile up. The database records the difference between the date we receive an application and when we log it in the system.'

Joan's face darkened. She went to her desk and began to type. She hated and feared the database; Leela had been hired partly in order to keep its malevolence under control.

'Chai, kaapi?' said Tipu Sultan patiently. His name was not Tipu Sultan but Chhotu. It can't have been Chhotu either, but that is what everyone other than Sathya called him. Sathya, in his friendly, offensive way, had decided the boy, an ageing perpetual adolescent, looked like Tipu Sultan because of his twirly moustache. He could be jocularly rude to the tea boy but also, Leela found out much later, paid his fees to go to an evening class and get a diploma in basic computer studies, one of the many kindnesses he concealed from general view.

'Coffee, do, strong,' Leela said. He held out the wire tray; she chose two darker looking glasses. When Sathya returned he would take out the tin of Nescafé from his desk, and offer

Leela a supplementary spoon, murmuring, 'Bilge ... look at us, like addicts.'

The ancient standing fan turned her way. A strong breath hit her shoulders and neck, and blew her hair aside. She sighed, enjoying it, hung onto her papers. When it had passed she looked down again.

Application for grant. Name of body making application: Nritya Dance Trust. Date of application: 2nd February 2004.

She heard Sathya exhale. In the background, Joan was quarrelling on the telephone.

Leela opened a new record in the database. She hated its interface, ugly and grey, and the clunky buttons on screen. She continually had to pay attention to it, which she disliked, yet there was no way of shining at her work.

A bird sang outside; a crow cawed. At twelve, she would be starving. Tipu Sultan would come around again, with tea. She'd drink it, and turn her stomach.

At one thirty, Joan went to the canteen to meet a friend. Leela had tried but failed to imagine her having actual conversation with anyone. Perhaps instead she and her friend simply complained at each other.

Sathya would sigh, and get out his paper and the tiffin his mother sent for him. He was in his forties, grizzled and plump, and lived with his parents. They periodically tried, he said, to marry him off. 'Who the hell would want to marry me?' he enquired of Leela, who said, 'Er, there must be people ...'

'I'm happy,' said Sathya. 'I have companionship, I have my interests.' Leela envied him.

She picked up her bag when Joan had left for lunch. 'Go,' Sathya said with a wink. He said he told Joan, whenever she returned, that Leela had just left. But Leela was often back within half an hour, for she had little purpose. She began by hurrying down the stairs, with their red-earth spittle stains and stencilled notices (Do Not Spit), and emerged below into the short lane where yellow school buses were parked.

Bougainvillea, hot pink and orange, hung over the school walls. Expensive cars and their drivers waited; some drivers held tiffins. The lane was dusty and hot. She hurried through the waiting people.

Sometimes, she wandered into the Khadi Bhavan. It remained a temple to the Gandhian nation that seemed never quite to have come into being. Its dark wood counters still held rolls of khadi, some fine and soft as voile; there were displays of ahimsak chappals made from the hide of cows that had died a natural death. Upstairs, the gifts: puppets from Rajasthan, bags from Gujarat, rosewood and ivory elephants, things made of sandalwood. She knew, thanks to her father, that kantha saris were beautiful, and could tell in which ones the work was good; she could admire bedspreads of kalam-kari or blockprint. She moved through the sections with a borrowed expression of knowledge tinged with cynicism.

Today she stopped at a counter of wooden toys and picked up a painted cup with a handle, attached by string to a wooden ball. She and her sister had once been given a pair of these, the sort of handcrafted toys one's parents' friends thought were charming. Leela had carried hers around for a while, pretending to play with it; Neeti had broken hers at once and looked happy.

'Where are these from?' she asked the salesman.

He eyed her. 'Madhya Pradesh.'

'Can I see that?' She pointed at a pink Ganpati.

He brought it down. Gingerly, she turned two of its rounded arms, one ending in a hand bearing a laddoo, the other upraised, palm flat in benediction. They moved cheerfully.

'Here.' The salesman took the idol from her and turned the arms more vigorously. There was another pair behind them, one carrying a mace, one a snare.

'These ones don't move?'

'No,' he said. He gave her back the statue. The god sat on a dark pink base, where a tiny mouse was painted.

'How much is it?'

He turned it over. 'Hundred fifteen.'

At the hostel she removed the stapled paper bag. The pink Ganpati came out. She dusted him, put him on top of the small bookshelf, and after her bath said her prayer in front of him; he afterwards looked quite as pleased as before.

23

Chitra and her roommate finished listening to Leela complain after dinner. She was sick of men bumping into her on purpose, or punching her in the breast when she walked home. She couldn't understand why everyone was so unfriendly. Everything was complicated. Going to the bank took ages.

'Why did you come back? I don't understand,' Chitra said. She started to laugh; she had a big laugh.

'I thought Bombay was some kind of lost home. I thought I'd find that missing sense of belonging here. It sounds insane,' Leela admitted. She heard herself say it and giggled; it was so boring. 'I can't remember. But how did we get here, of all places?' All three looked at the fluorescent-lit dining hall, the formica tables, the shutter to the kitchen, which Datta, the handsome, Byronic cook, was now shutting with a great clatter. He began to wipe it energetically.

'We should go,' Shobha said. She laughed. 'I think he wants us to.'

'Come to our room,' Chitra said.

Leela's heart leapt. 'Aren't you busy?'

'With what?'

They shared a room on the same floor as hers, larger than her room and with two single beds. 'This is nice,' she said, wondering if she would have been able to bear sharing. Shobha was very sweet. Yet how would Leela have managed without being able to shut the door of her room, and silently rage about the world and its failure to welcome her? 'Did you know each other before?' she asked.

'No, we just met a few months ago,' Chitra said. 'I've only been back a few months.'

'Oh?'

'You know how you get three years, then you have to move out?'

'Yeah.'

'But if it's been more than three years since you left you can do another term.'

'Oh.'

'I didn't complete my last term. It was just a few months.' Chitra looked angry now. Leela was confused. 'I was at home for a while.'

'Then you came back?'

'Then I came back.'

'And she became my roomie!' Shobha, who was smaller and thinner, came to wrap her arms around Chitra and hug her. The two of them beamed at a startled Leela. Chitra said later, resigned, and when they were alone, 'I wanted to live in a single. I begged them. And my income was the right level. But they decided to put me with a roommate. Shobha's a sweetie, it's not that.' Her face darkened. 'My father had just died when I came back, and I was engaged but it fell through. There were some weekends I didn't get out of bed at all. I think Pawar wanted to make sure I wasn't alone.'

Shobha brought out some chocolate. They pressed it on Leela, who didn't want to cut into the precious supply.

'Go on,' said Chitra. 'You don't have to worry about your weight.'

'I'm trying to put on weight,' said Shobha.

Leela was amused. 'Well, I think I have been putting on weight. I keep buying myself little bags of Gems after dinner. I don't even know why.'

'You're lonely,' said Chitra.

Leela was embarrassed. 'Maybe.'

'What do you do, Leela?' Shobha asked.

Leela told them how she'd applied for jobs, and put up her CV on a website for the non-profit sector. 'It's terribly paid, it's for the Sohrab Trust.'

'I've heard of them, of course.'

'I look after the grant applications, write some stuff for the website, that sort of thing.'

Shobha worked in a corporate law firm. 'The hours are crazy,' she said.

'She's out of hostel at seven sometimes,' Chitra said. 'Not back till after ten.'

They carried on talking, about their lives and families, making jokes. Leela sat straight-backed on Shobha's bed and waited for the inevitable slackening of conversation.

'I'm exhausted,' Chitra said.

'It might be bedtime,' Shobha said. She smiled at Leela.

'Of course. Good night!' She hurried to the door. In the corridor, and in her room, checking the time – a quarter past ten – she was warm with embarrassment. She should have left earlier; no wonder she wasn't making friends.

She took to going home every other weekend. She left the hostel when it was just becoming light, and took the bus on empty roads to the station. In the ladies compartment, she'd watch the scenery for ten minutes as they rolled out of the city, slum upon well-established slum. Then she'd fall into a deep swoon, neck jolting this way and that. Near Pune, she'd reawaken, often as the train passed Shivajinagar. She'd rub her eyes and roll her neck as they pulled into the city.

For a while those trips kept her sane amid her anxiety about conforming to a world whose rules she didn't understand, either because there weren't any, or because they were too multi-layered, a cascading interdependent set of priorities.

Her parents were misfits too, she recalled. In their home, faced with her mother's angst about the availability of broccoli, or sprouts that could be trusted ('but think of the water they must've used'), or tofu, or wheat-free biscuits, and her father's gently irrelevant conversation, and both of their lack of engagement with the world around them – her father would drift over to turn on the World Service television channel, rather than watch the news on a local channel – she could bask in their collective strangeness, their being, as a family, out of joint with the times.

She'd arrive, blasted with tiredness, eyes rubbed with sleep, in the morning, say hello to her parents and the bai and the cook and sit in the living room talking to her father or alone with the papers till the cook finished in a flurry of cleaning the kitchen and putting saucepans away and she and the bai smiled and left together.

There would be relative silence, and peace. They'd have lunch, and elliptically discuss their states of mind, though never in the thorough way she'd observed in other people's families: how have you been, or how did this or that go? When she was younger, she had resented the apparent lack of interest. She would go home then and try to follow her mother around, telling her what had happened in college and the events of her and her friends' lives. Mrs Ghosh would listen for a while but respond by asking not 'How did you feel?' or 'What happened then?' but, 'Have you thought about an internship, darling?' or 'What are your plans for when you graduate?' Her father, when Leela directed her conversation at him, would also listen for a while then, so mildly that it was hard to be openly angry about it, his hand would find itself reaching for a magazine or the book in which he was presently immersed. His face, if Leela complained, was a mix of sympathy (ostensibly for her but really, she knew, for himself) and wheedling apology. 'You're not listening, Baba!' she'd point out, and he, still clutching the book or magazine, would say plaintively, 'But Leela, I've been listening to you for *twenty minutes* now.'

Some months after the first monsoon, when she was beginning to accept her life, and looked less than once a week at the unused portion of her return air ticket, there was a week when she lost her appetite. She felt feverish, bright with energy, and raced around at work. Every time she sat down to eat, a wave of nausea rose in her.

'I feel sick,' she confessed to Sathya when they went out for a dosa, as they now did every few weeks. 'Some sort of bug.'

He looked at her attentively. 'Pull your lower eyelid down. Look up. Hmm. How's your pee?'

'What?'

'Is it brown?'

'No!'

He shook his head. 'Better go see a doctor first thing.'

She went to the sardonic, expensive GP everyone in the hostel saw. 'Get a urine test if you want,' he said, 'but I'm telling you it's jaundice.'

The next day, with the test results, she called Sathya. 'Poor bastard,' he said. 'Better call Joan.'

Leela called Joan. 'Oh *no*,' said Joan.

'Four to six weeks,' said Leela, not without satisfaction.

24

Her father came into her room with a steel plate; on it, chunks of peeled sugar cane. 'Akash got it for you.' Akash was the driver. 'It's black ganna. He said to eat it first thing, even before you touch water.' She sat up.

Every morning she went to the pathology lab for a blood test. Once a week she took the reports to the doctor. Her bilirubin went up, then down. She became unreasoningly hungry, and lay in bed eating toast and reading long, undemanding books.

The office fell away. She dreamt sometimes of a detail of her life there, and would wake to think of its unreality: the database, or an email about a meeting to discuss the way the city's parks were being taken over by private businesses. Sathya phoned once or twice, to ask where Leela had filed a particular record, then to tell her of Joan's latest annoying habit. 'When are you coming back to the freak show?' he asked, almost without curiosity.

She wrote to Amy, and other friends, but heard back only sporadically. It was as though she were between worlds; no longer part of the London life she had exited, nor her new life.

As the weeks passed, she wandered about the house in the afternoons, watched squirrels duel in the trees outside, and later walked in the lanes around the building, looking in at the crumbling summer houses, and the bored watchmen sitting outside them. Five weeks after she had come home, she felt more energetic, more restless. She went out with her mother to buy clothes; Mrs Ghosh said Leela looked too scruffy for someone working in an office. She accompanied her father on his stroll in the evening. She read a new novel. She called Sathya, and asked him to tell Joan she'd be in the office on Monday.

25

She had thought to go upstairs quietly at the hostel, but Pawar spotted her. 'Leela Ghosh!' she called out. She was smiling.

'Hello ma'am,' said Leela, forgetting to resist. Five o'clock, Sunday evening, everyone was in the hostel, either flitting in or on their way out. Pawar got up and put an arm around Leela. 'Are you better? Patli toh ho gayi.'

'I don't think I've lost weight,' Leela said.

'You've reduced,' Pawar said firmly.

Chitra appeared and let out a squeal. 'You're back!'

Leela was dazzled. 'Hi,' she said.

'You've really lost weight. How are you feeling?'

'I'm okay, I'm fine now.'

A couple of other girls that she sometimes talked to at meals stopped to smile and ask after her.

'You probably just want to take your stuff up, no?' Chitra said. 'I'll call the lift.'

The 'Für Elise' halted, they jolted up. Leela inhaled. 'The hostel smell,' she said. 'I'd forgotten it.'

'Eau de Phenyl?'

She was lost in an evocation of the dark, cool corridors, the doors of different rooms, and hers among them, on the left towards the end: single room with sea view which, as Pawar said, made her a very lucky girl.

They came to the seventh floor. 'Do you need a hand unpacking, babe?'

'No, I'll be fine,' Leela said.

'See you at dinner? Eight thirty?' Chitra said.

'Great.'

Leela trundled her bag along the corridor, took out her key and opened the door. The room was clean, peculiarly familiar. The window and balcony door were closed; it was too warm. She turned on the fan. The desk was neat, but otherwise, with her bedspread on the bed, the pink Ganpati on top of the bookshelf, dusty but undamaged, the room looked as though she had walked out of it a day or two earlier; as though the last month had simply not happened.

She woke early, and walked to work, enjoying the exercise and the sense of leisure. She was one of the first people in the building; the watchman didn't recognise her at first and she had to show him her identity card. She went up to the office and began to open her mail.

Sathya found her when he arrived. 'Hey!' he cried joyously. 'You're back.'

She grinned. But he bustled about his desk. 'She's going crazy about something. Just let me sort these out. I need to make a call.' Ten minutes later, he got up when Tipu Sultan came in, and said, 'Come, let's go for a cigarette?'

They stood outside in the stone stairwell, moving out of the way for peons carrying twenty-litre bottles of mineral water, or chairs with broken seats.

'So you're okay? Feeling better now?' Sathya asked. 'You look thinner. You look good though.'

Leela grinned and rolled her eyes. 'Thanks.'

'I feel it's important to say these things,' said Sathya, grinning back. 'When are you going to get a boyfriend?'

Leela was mildly affronted. 'Next week, is it on my task list?' Joan had decided Sathya and Leela should draw up weekly task lists and prioritise their to-dos on a whiteboard.

'It should be. You're young and attractive. Don't turn into me.'

'Is it that bad?' Leela had never arrived satisfactorily at a conclusion about whether Sathya was attracted to her. Residually perhaps – they got on very well. But with any serious intent? To her chagrin, she thought not, though when she imagined anything actually happening between them, she froze in horror.

'Try not to look absolutely appalled.'

'No, no, I didn't mean that.' She touched his arm in apology.

'I don't actually feel bad about it,' he said. 'I don't want to get married, which is apparently the only relationship option in this fucking country.'

'Hm, no? Maybe you haven't found the right person?'

'Every woman wants to get married. If I'm with someone, I want to see her three times a week. Maybe twice. I like my life. I'm not desperate to get married.'

Leela regarded him dubiously. She looked at the smouldering paper stick in her hand. 'I can't finish this. It's making me sick. Sorry.' She stubbed it out in the paper-filled ashtray.

Sathya raised an eyebrow. 'You probably shouldn't smoke anyway. What about your liver?'

'What about my liver,' she repeated. Just the grey curls of smoke floating in the stairwell made her queasy.

'Let's go for a drink one night this week,' Sathya said.

'Drink?'

'You can eat peanuts and watch me drink. Which is pretty much all you ever do.'

'I'll drink whisky.'

'You do that.' He put out his cigarette.

Leela thought that evening, as she lay on her bed listening to the crows and gulls outside, that it was as though she had been reborn. She walked cleanly through the city every morning, woke earlier, felt lighter. Things seemed to have fallen away.

On Thursday she and Sathya sat in Leo's bar. A waiter sidled towards them. 'Another beer, sir?'

'Another beer?' Sathya asked himself. He examined the bottle on the table. 'No, not yet,' he said. 'Do you want another, whatever rubbish you're drinking?'

'No,' Leela said. After her third fresh lime soda (sweet) she'd realised matching Sathya drink for drink would make her feel burpy and sick.

'Hm,' said Sathya. 'Well, this is exciting.'

'Can you ask him for more saltines?'

He waved at the waiter. 'Bring her more of those things.'

The waiter departed, nodding.

'So, how long are you going to stay in this ridiculous job?'

'What else should I do?' she asked.

A large, quite drunk black man began to dance slowly on the tiny, sticky dance area under the single disco ball. He seemed to be moving to a song different from the one playing.

'Christ,' said Sathya. 'Look at him.'

'He looks like he's having fun.' She accepted a fresh bowl of saltines from the waiter.

'Probably. Do you think we should be doing that? Should we take some of whatever he's had? Isn't this the place to get hold of all of that?'

'Is it?'

'Of course. Colaba. Firangs. Don't you know these things, in your hostel?'

Leela sighed. 'The hostel's really not like that.'

'I bet. Anyway, how long are you going to carry on like this?'

'Like what?'

The man stopped dancing and leaned against the edge of the DJ booth. He called over a waiter.

'Pointless job, living in hostel.'

'Thanks.'

'You know what I mean.'

'What else should I be doing?'

'How could I possibly know? You must be passionate about something.'

Leela looked at him. His eyes were slightly red; it was smoky inside, despite the fierce air conditioning.

'Books, maybe.'

'Journalism? Publishing?'

'Maybe.'

'Marriage?'

'Oh, fuck off.'

He raised an eyebrow and grinned.

'What about *you*?' enquired Leela.

'What about me?'

'How can you not be married?'

'Because I'm so rich and attractive?'

'I was thinking of your age, actually.'

He guffawed. 'I told you, I don't want to. At least I don't want to get married to the kind of woman I could probably still get married to.'

'Matrimonials?'

'Fuck that – tall fair high caste engineer?'

'Homely. Divorce no bar.'

He laughed again. 'What about indifference no bar?'

Leela looked at him dubiously.

'I'm not gay, if that's what you're thinking.'

'I don't mind either way,' she pointed out.

'How sweet. No, but I'm not. I'd probably get laid more if I were. Look, there was some female, okay, if you want to know. In Bangalore, of all places. Very nice, attractive, just a bit crazy.'

'When was this?'

'About nine months ago.'

'What's her name?'

'Meenakshi.'

'Ooh, I like the name. Doesn't it mean fish-eyed?' The meaning of names was a speciality of her father's.

'It means pain in the ass as far as I recall.'

'Oh, really?'

'No, no.' Sathya put down his glass slightly too hard and spilt some beer. Leela giggled. 'No,' he went on, 'the point was that she was very attractive, it was very nice, being able to have sex was great. But then she wanted to get married, and I wasn't too sure. She wanted to live separately. I live with my parents.'

'Couldn't you have lived near them or something?'

He went off on his usual rant about independence.

'I wish I felt like that,' Leela said.

'You're a nice normal girl.'

'Are you being sarcastic?'

'No, I mean it. Everything will work out. It has to. You need to meet some people. Go out.'

'I am out.'

'Not with me. Let me think,' Sathya said, 'if I know anyone.'

'What about him? Shall I fall in love with him?' She indicated the man in white, who was now off the dance floor, in a booth, still alone, looking grumpy.

'Maybe. He does look a bit like a drug dealer, but if you don't mind that.'

'It might as well be him. It could be anyone, you know? Have you ever thought that?' Leela said suddenly. 'You know, when you fall in love, the randomness of it? Like a feeling is just waiting to get attached to a person? Have you ever thought: Who'll be the next person to come along and make me unhappy? You know how when you're in love, you get obsessed with that person and think you see them everywhere? When it's not them? And then when the person who isn't them comes nearer, you realise they're not even attractive? But you thought they were the person you're obsessed with? What does that mean? Does it mean the person you're in love with isn't even as amazing as you think? Like there was this guy I liked, he had dark hair and a beard and every time I saw a man with a beard out of the corner of my eye I'd think: it's him. But it wouldn't be – and it'd be someone really unattractive, and then I'd feel strange. What if I was even wrong about him being attractive?' She finished the saltines. 'You know?'

Sathya looked at her disbelievingly, then guffawed. 'You can be this intense on fresh lime soda? Have a drink.'

'I can't, I just had jaundice.'

'You should be careful,' he said automatically. 'Don't want to have a relapse.' He drained his beer, waved at the waiter, and made a gesture of one hand writing on another. 'I should go, catch the train. Come, I'll drop you.'

'It's not on the way.'

'It'll take ten minutes.'

The waiter came over. Sathya examined the bill.

'How much?' Leela asked.

'Shut up. You weren't even drinking. Come on, let's go, unless you want to talk to your friend over there.'

The man in white had his forearms on the table; his head rested on them.

She wasn't going home this weekend, the first since her return; but her sense of anticipation had drizzled away. Joan had asked on Friday, though cautiously, since Leela had at first fiercely refused such demands, 'There's a meeting for Citiwatch in the evening, on Sunday, at six, can you go?'

'Where –'

'It's in Colaba. Just pop in, be there for twenty minutes. Take some cards.' Leela had recently acquired business cards.

'Okay,' Leela said.

'Wonderful. I'll give you the address. Oh, it's in Cuffe Parade – even closer.'

On Sunday, she was pleased to have the appointment. She had spent the previous day walking around, eating dosa and reading, and had woken early, not tired. The day passed pleasantly: the usual lull of breakfast, the paper, a walk out to check her email, buy some laundry detergent and shampoo. Back in her room, she looked around her and wondered at her life. The rusty table, painted annually in the hostel store with black galvanised paint; the cupboard, the clean but chipped cement and marble-chip tiles, the wooden bed and formica desk. All surfaces in the hostel were wipe-clean where possible; it wasn't always. Just before Leela had become ill, one Monday morning the dining room had been hushed at breakfast. When she wondered why, Chitra told her that an older woman some of them knew had died in her room that weekend. She was in her late thirties and turned out to have been epileptic; she had had a fit and died without anyone realising till the next day.

Leela had recalled the perfunctory medical exam she'd had to undergo before being admitted to the hostel.

'I guess they didn't know,' Chitra said. 'Can you imagine, dying like that? The bai said there was blood all over the walls.'

'No one heard?' Leela felt her mouth become salty.

'Saturday afternoon, I guess everyone was out.'

Now Leela imagined a man, perhaps the kitchen manager or someone else, supervised by the punctilious hostel accountant, collecting the furniture from that room and having it repainted, and the bai who must have gone in to clean away death from the walls. Still, she couldn't feel it was a failure of the hostel and its uniform, provisional way of life, whose temporariness she enjoyed. But would you be happy, she argued with herself, as she watched a football game below in the lane, if you lived like this for ever, if you could? With the same job, the same life? Without possessions, an apartment of your own, children – but the children were indistinct. It was the fear of not having the things others had, rather than the desire for those things.

Sitting in the door with her mug of orange tea, she lost track of time. The sky paled, and a smoke-like darkness began to smudge it. No time to think about what to wear. She changed quickly and left the hostel as dusk fell.

The meeting was in a building near the Colaba Woods, a long tree-lined park around which some elderly men and a woman were walking. It had an Arthurian name she couldn't remember. Guinevere? Lancelot? Camelot, that was it; a Deco building with a low, wrought-iron gate and trees behind the wall. Who calls a building Camelot, she thought, but remembered having a friend, when very young, who lived in a dusty Deco building in Colaba called Hampton Court.

'Agarwal,' she said to the watchman who stopped her near the gate.

He nodded.

Leela waited for the lift, with a middle-aged woman and a young man. The woman was talking. The man, Leela thought, must be her son, though she was so much smaller, and elegantly dressed where he was tall, bearded, not unhandsome, but with a linen or khadi shirt not quite tucked in, and slightly crumpled chinos.

'Probably darling, but that isn't the point,' the older woman was saying. 'You've been back for a couple of months now, you should get involved with something, at least reconnect with people.'

Her voice remained soft even as it insisted, in a way that impressed Leela. But when the other woman turned a quizzical face towards her, she looked down at her worn chappals and was embarrassed. This would have been a good moment to introduce herself, and say something in a loud, confident voice. The presence of the young man, and the woman's elegance – she wore a short, dusty pink silk kurta, white pyjamas, and dull gold ear studs that Leela liked against her silver hair – made her remain silent.

The lift came, and the young man opened the door. He waited first for his mother, then for Leela, and the thought came to her and made her smile with its unexpectedness, that he would often be opening doors for his mother and her, and that at some time she might tire of it.

'Which floor?' the older woman asked. She looked at Leela.

'Two please.'

She pressed only the second button; they all got out together.

'Are you going to the Agarwal house?'

'Yes. Are you going to the Citiwatch meeting?'

'Yes, yes.' The other woman laughed; she seemed to be amused by the question.

'Er, I'm Leela Ghosh, I work at the Sohrab Trust.'

'Oh? With whom?'

'Joan Mascarenhas.'

'I know Joan. I didn't know there was someone else there now. Has Radha left?'

'She went to London, she works in an auction house.'

The young man was ringing the doorbell. As footsteps came towards it, Leela was saying, 'I've only been there a year – not quite.'

A woman opened the door and pounced on them. 'Welcome, welcome, come in! Shalini, Vikram, how are you? My God, you're looking so handsome and grown up!'

Leela smiled behind them, wondered whether to remove her sandals, didn't see any at the door, regretted briefly having worn the kolhapuris in which she walked everywhere, and drifted uncertainly past the hall, the open doorway to the kitchen – a bearer looked out – and into the drawing room.

Knots of people, mostly women of a certain age and income, had gathered and were talking with enthusiasm around different focal points: a marble planter that might have come off the set of a Pirandello play; a side table that held a large bronze Natraj; and a walnut sideboard on which stood a silver tray and bottles of liquor. Next to it, a small, reproving looking man in white uniform of short-sleeved bush shirt and trousers, his hair neatly oiled, his spectacles of wire. Leela looked on as a taller, baggier man, his beard silver, came up to say something to the bearer, then watch him administer a drink, whisky with several ice cubes.

'May I help you?' A large lady in a loud, printed silk blouse and slacks came up. Bits of her blinged: earrings, buttons, shiny discs on her sandals. Leela liked her on principle, but felt tired and exasperated at always being the person who, by dint of scruffiness, or youth, or not being known, must be addressed in this slightly hectoring way. She smiled.

'I'm Leela Ghosh, from the Sohrab Trust. Joan Mascarenhas asked me to come along and say hello.'

'Ah, you're Leeeeeela!' Leela felt sure this lady had not before been aware of her existence. 'I'm Shilpa Agarwal.'

'Hello,' simpered Leela.

'So lovely to meet you Leela. Now, I hear a bit of an accent. Where are you from?'

'I've spent some time in England,' Leela said.

'Oh really? Where did you do your college?'

'Cambridge.'

'How wonderful!' Mrs Agarwal was steering Leela through the crowd. 'Tea?' They stopped at a table with a tea and perhaps a coffee pot on it.

'Is there any coffee?'

'Of course. Milk? Sugar?'

'Just sugar please.'

When Leela had a cup of coffee, Shilpa Agarwal got a plate and put two bhajias and a canapé on it despite Leela's demurrals. 'Veg? Really? That's interesting.' She steered Leela further into a corner. 'Now, what do you know about Citiwatch?'

'Well, of course, I know about your campaign for safer road crossings,' Leela said, dredging this from a memory of a newspaper article some months earlier.

'Ah yes. Well! We are an organisation formed by several friends, *concerned citizens* you might say, in 1997, in order to really *do something* about the city. We love Mumbai, Leela.'

'Yes, yes,' Leela agreed. She let herself go glazed and limp under the speech that followed, in which she also made mental notes for future reference: parks, open spaces, citizens' action.

Before Shilpa seemed to have drawn to a conclusion, she became bored. 'Leela, just *one minute*, someone I must speak to over there.' Leela agreed and was left standing next to a corner table. She was out of the flow of the room, to her relief, and stood near a sofa with claw-ball feet; she looked sideways out of the window and wondered how soon she could leave.

'Hi,' said a voice. Lurking not far away was the tall, bearded young man of the lift.

'Oh, hi.'

He leaned a bit towards her, apparently less a gesture than a habitual, courtly tropism. 'What's your name?'

'Leela. What's yours?'

'Vikram. Vikram Sahni.'

She smiled aggressively at him.

He grinned back. 'So you're here for work.'

'Yes.'

'Do you enjoy these occasions very much?'

She grinned. His voice was soft, its inflections more neutral than most people's. 'Yes, they're my favourite thing.'

He smiled, apparently quite guilelessly. 'I thought they must be.'

'What about you, why are you here?'

He nodded towards the colourful figure of Shilpa Agarwal some yards away. 'Family friend. My mother's also involved.'

'In Citiwatch?'

'Mm.' He nodded. 'They do some good things, civic work.'

'Of course,' said Leela, a bit embarrassed.

'But these occasions are slightly deadly.'

She gave a cautious smile.

'They're the sort of thing,' he went on, 'that makes me wish I'd stayed in my bedroom and disappeared.'

She looked at him a bit irritably and waited.

'A headstand. I call it my disappearing act.'

'A yoga headstand?'

He nodded. 'I've only been doing it for a year or so.'

'Unsupported?' asked Leela.

'Haan.'

She was envious. 'Why disappearing act?'

He grinned again. His teeth were large, whitish. 'Your mind goes blank. Like in meditation, but it's more of a physical effect in the sirsasana.'

'No thoughts?'

'Some. Not many though. It's quiet, in a different way from just, you know, being quiet. Reading or something. It's not like that.'

She nodded, and watched his face for clues about this interesting subject. He had a confiding manner; she already felt less estranged from him than from most people. He was tall, well made, in the French expression, and not from going to a gym but probably from a childhood of regular sport. Some nostalgia arose in her for the time of order that his body represented.

He was looking at her, but she couldn't read his expression. 'I go to this meditation group sometimes. You could come if you wanted, it's open to everyone.'

'Is it a specific method?'

'Not really. It has a link with the Pondicherry ashram. But it's just a place where people go to meditate together. It's nice.'

'Where does it happen?'

'Near Churchgate. Monday afternoon, usually, but late. When do you – I suppose you'd be at work?'

'Oh, I can probably get out of the office. I finish at five thirty-six but I can get out earlier once in a while.'

'They do it on Saturday afternoons too. Do you work on Saturday?'

'No.' She shook her head quickly and smiled in mock shame.

'I could put you on the mailing list. What's your email address?'

His mother appeared. 'Darling, we need to leave now if we're going to get home in time to change before we go out.'

Leela started, as though caught out. She smiled a social smile at Mrs Sahni, who looked back at her, then smiled quickly and charmingly.

'Ah, oh, okay,' said Vikram. 'Mummy, do you have pen-paper?'

'Just a minute.' She had glasses on, and began to rummage in her small, elegant bag.

'No, it's okay,' said Leela. 'I have a card.'

Mrs Sahni stopped and stared.

'Ah, sorry. I mean –'

'Leela is interested in our meditation group,' Vikram said without embarrassment. 'Give me a card,' he told Leela.

She gave him a card. Mrs Sahni was still examining her.

'All right, darling?' she asked her son, and smiled at Leela.

'Bye,' he said to Leela. He put out a hand, and its largeness and warmth enclosed hers for a moment, then he loped off with his small mother without looking back.

26

'More coffee?'

'No.' Leela unfolded her legs. 'I have to go.'

'I'll walk you back,' Vikram said. They got down from the marble ledge where they'd been sitting next to the open window, a mosquito gadget behind her burning its sweetish-smelling tablet.

Not since she'd been in Bombay had she found this kind of friendship: a relaxed expanse of time spent with someone, sometimes eating or drinking beer, but mostly talking. There was an eagerness about him that she had to respond to.

They went down in the lift and out of the lobby, the somnolent watchman rising from his stool as they came out. The night was warm as bath water. They rounded the corner, where heavy bougainvillea spilled over a wall. 'This corner makes me think of Pondy. Honestly, Leela, you should go to Pondy.' He was smoking a cigarette and threw the end at the base of the wall.

'Pondicherry?'

'Go to the ashram. It's a great place. Just to walk around – it's like the quiet parts of Colaba but quieter. Cleaner. A great place to meditate or just be.'

'Shouldn't you be able to meditate anywhere?'

'Yeah, in theory, but some places …' His attention was always wandering; it would come to a point, though it was hard to predict what made him pause; then it would drift. But when it did pause, there was an intensity that she liked.

They walked down a side lane, past a hotel, an attar shop, a bundle of human being sleeping in a doorway, someone smoking near a cigarette stall. A rat was busy in the gutter.

The sound of their chappals, the swish of her trouser hems against each other, brought back an early memory: her father taking her to school in the rains, the legs of his corduroy trousers singing as they brushed each other; the sound and the need for hurry; the green, guttery smell of the rain.

At the hostel, Vikram said a brief goodbye at the last streetlamp before the gate. He didn't linger. Last week, she'd tried to give him a hug, and he'd stood, patient but board-like, before smiling and leaving. He always waited until she walked into the gate. Leela, embarrassed, would avoid the eyes of the older nightwatchman, who sat on his stool late at night singing his prayers. She'd go in, sign the register, get her mail, and walk up the stairs: the lift was shut off at ten.

The fluorescent light of her room would be transformed against the darkness, and she'd sit on her bed, staring through the window, or stand on the balcony, feeling the night and its warmth, and the small distance from the room where she'd been talking to Vikram. The city stopped being an entity in itself; it became a backdrop.

On Monday afternoon for the fourth week running she loitered outside a building on A road, Churchgate. Opposite, a college or club had a dowdy sign; people filed in and out. Cars jostled for parking space.

'Ah, hey, sorry, come, let's go up.' Vikram arrived; his hand was briefly on her shoulder. They started up the stairs, and stopped at the third floor. One door was slightly ajar, and outside it there were several sets of slippers.

She would think of the room later and wonder about her nervousness the first time she'd walked in. That persisted for a while; then it became usual, and the lack of surprise was something to flaunt. She'd drop her chappals near the door, breeze in, and go to her favourite space near the back, by the window. A sliver of sunlight got in through the blinds. Fans were on. You could hear traffic.

A man in white kurta-pyjama got up and went to the altar at the front of the room, where there were flowers and a picture of the Mother and Sri Aurobindo. He lit bunches of incense sticks, and a heady scent of flowers filled the room. People closed their eyes.

Leela closed hers too. She sat a metre behind Vikram. Sometimes he was on her left, or they were separated by another person. He became remote, still. She had at first found it threatening, looked to him for a response, but there was none, and she'd concentrated instead on appearing to be so lost in her meditation that she was unaware of the outside world. This made her more antsy than usual, but it was pleasant to open her eyes and watch people fidget, feel the silence, or gaze out of the window, unobserved, except when one of the facilitators saw her and discreetly looked away.

When her eyes were closed, her thoughts sprinted. She thought of Vikram, in a heated, hurried way. Did he like her?

How much? What would happen between them? She needed to know as soon as possible; at the same time, she found it difficult to envisage change. Time passed; just as she slipped into unawareness of herself, someone would rustle to the front and ring the bell.

The first time, she and Vikram had ended up walking home, until their paths diverged, when he'd said with some embarrassment, 'Well, I have to go this way.'

'See you,' Leela had said, sounding to herself like Richard.

Today she waited outside for him, examining the traffic. It had calmed. The sea at the end of the street sent a haze into the sky. She had an urge to walk along the wide pavement of Marine Drive, then sit on the sun-warmed ledge. When she had first come to Bombay, or come back, in the evenings after work she used to walk here. She had felt embarrassed to be alone, but less than in many places; and she had liked the weird, democratic streams of people passing each way, either walking for exercise, or dawdling, or sitting, or canoodling, or laughing, or looking at girls. Many people sat with their backs to the sea, facing the traffic. There were the south Bombayites, those who lived perhaps in Chowpatty or Malabar Hill or Colaba. And there were poor students, feral-eyed young people conducting love affairs in low tones, sitting very close together.

'Do you want to go for coffee?' Vikram had come down. He stood next to her, tall and apparently belonging to the part of the world that had sense and place, not whimsy; she admired his worn, short-sleeved cotton shirt, his sandals and the past summers they evoked.

'Can we – I want to go for a walk on Marine Drive. For a bit anyway.'

'Okay,' he said. They passed parked cars, taxis, and the quiet Deco blocks set back from the road. At the main road they waited to cross.

Every time she saw the sea she felt glad, as though its movement expressed a secret blitheness that allowed the city to continue. The city without sight of the sea was serious, a determined climbing up narrow ladders to opportunity, but with anxiety, commuters pushing away others.

Vikram raised his eyebrows at her and smiled.

'I like the way the sea makes you forget anything serious,' she said. They were walking slowly in the direction of Girgaum.

'How do you mean?'

'It's playful.'

'The sea? I suppose it depends. Not when you're on it. Not for fishermen.' His white shirt flapped against him.

'Fishermen.' She smiled. 'But its movement, the way it's always in motion.' She walked, feeling the thin chappals hit the warm tarmac. The breeze struck her side-on and the last sun was on the large-leaved, odd trees that had been planted here some time, when? She didn't know. 'What are these trees anyway?'

'No idea. Some sort of badam?'

'They're weird. Weren't there coconut trees here once?'

'This end? I don't know.'

'I feel like …' She tailed off.

Vikram smiled. She knew he was amused by her determined love for the city.

'You feel like you're going to write a poem to the palm trees?'

'I feel like I'm going to throw a nariyal at anyone who says annoying things.'

'Let's sit.' He was one of those Bombayites who say they love to walk.

They found a spot on the wide, warm parapet and looked out to sea.

Leela took off her chappals, placed them beside her, felt paranoid about someone running off with one as a joke, and crossed her legs in a half-lotus. 'What do you really think about during meditation?' she asked.

He laughed mid-exhalation. 'You don't beat about the bush, do you?' In these old-fashioned idioms she thought she heard his original accent, rather than the neutral, sometimes American-inflected, sometimes English accent in which he ordinarily spoke.

She stared out towards Walkeshwar. The sun was orange, sinking, the sky flared peach. There were houses down there, at the water's edge, but they were small. At the end of the peninsula, the Governor's land.

'Well?'

'A lot of things, distraction. I try to empty my mind. You're a funny girl,' he said. 'Sometimes I think about you.'

Leela, her stomach jumping, was afraid to turn, but not only out of maidenish diffidence. 'About me?'

His face was unreadable, still handsome, tanned, apparently candid. 'Among other things.'

'Oh.'

'You cross my mind.'

'Right, right.' She became aware of being uncomfortable, and changed legs.

'You do yoga?'

'Why?'

'That's an asana.'

'Not a real one.' She looked down at the sea, and also the tide going out, the dirty beach below. All kinds of rubbish: a rope that had once been a plastic bag, grit, the wrapper from a bag of chips, a tampon that they both looked away from at the same time. 'I used to do some yoga in London, and a bit when I was a child. My father practises, or used to. But it was very irritating. He'd keep telling me to do it every time I got stressed out, he'd say, you shouldn't get so worked up, why don't you learn yoga, that in itself put me off for a long time.'

He was grinning.

'I did some Iyengar classes for a while,' she went on, 'my flatmate was going to them. I do some stuff at the hostel, but I should get a book or something.'

'I have a book, a really simple one, from Pondy. It's old-fashioned, but it has all the basic asanas. You could take it.'

'Don't you need it?'

'I don't use it. I could get up and meet my mother's yoga teacher in the morning if I wanted. I'll find it for you. It has photographs, it's clear.'

'Okay.'

'My bottom has gone to sleep, do you want to see the sun set or what?'

'Or what.'

213

'We can if you want,' he said mildly, 'just say.'

'My bum's gone to sleep too,' Leela said. She felt tentative, but also pleased – he was prolonging the conversation, he had offered her the book.

They got up, Leela shaking stiff, heavy legs that seemed to belong to someone else.

'You want to go for coffee now?'

'Okay.'

27

One evening, when he was walking her home, he said, 'There's a party on Saturday, family friends, Juhu. Would you –? I'm going. If you wanted to it'd be nice.'

'You're asking me to go with you?'

'That's what I'm asking,' he said. 'It should be fun, a party after all. I'll pick you up if you want to go.'

His voice hadn't changed. She admired his calm, but couldn't tell if it originated in indifference, or a phlegmatic temperament. And there were practical considerations. Even a late pass at the hostel would only let her in till one o'clock, but it was embarrassing to point this out. 'Okay,' she said.

'About eight? It's early, I know, but there could be traffic.'

She nodded. They'd reached the streetlight.

'Oh, okay, so, well, great.'

She turned on her heel. 'Bye.'

She discussed it with Sathya the next day during a cigarette break.

'There's this guy. I see him a lot.'

'Ah? Something going on?'

'I don't know,' Leela said.

'Ah.' It seemed Sathya was not in an inquisitive mood.

'But I see him a lot,' Leela persisted.

He raised an eyebrow. 'You like him?'

'I think so.' She felt diffident and tried to sum up the case. 'He's attractive, nice, clever, he's studied abroad as well, we have things in common. I like spending time with him.'

'Ah ha. Doesn't sound like you like him,' he observed.

'I do. I mean –' She didn't want the conversation to end.

'So what's the problem?' Sathya stubbed out his cigarette in the sand of the large ashtray and turned to examine her. His eyes were a little red. She wondered if he did like her. Was she being insensitive?

'I can't tell what he feels.'

Sathya exhaled. 'He keeps coming to see you? Keeps wanting to meet?'

'Yeah, a few times a week.' She smiled.

He looked distracted. 'He's from Bombay? He lives at home here?'

'With his mother.'

His head went down. 'I think he must like you. Otherwise why go to all that effort? Come, let's go back.'

At the hostel, she tried and failed to catch Chitra for a longer conversation in which they could chew it over. On Saturday she slept in the afternoon, and woke in the early evening feeling disoriented. She rooted around in her cupboard, wondering what to wear. Her mother's voice returned to her. 'We need to do something about your clothes.' Most of what she owned was comfortable cotton garments for work. She put on jeans, kolhapuris and a silk top she hadn't worn since London.

At eight she hung about in the foyer. Fifteen minutes later Vikram arrived. He looked tall and laundered, an air of fresh shaving and a woody smelling cologne about him.

'You're ready?' he asked.

'Yep.'

'Here.' They walked out together, past a couple of inquisitive hostel girls, and into a cab he had waiting.

'You want to go to Juhu in this?' Leela asked. She tried to avoid taxis even for shorter journeys.

'I'm sorry I don't have the car, but we don't have a driver for the evenings right now, and there's no point driving to a party. I prefer not to drink and drive.'

'Of course, but what about the train? Wouldn't it be faster?'

Vikram gave her an odd look. He grinned. 'That's true. But I don't think we want to take the local to a party.'

Leela kept quiet. The taxi reached Marine Drive; it sat in traffic but she enjoyed the sulphurous fumes, the sparkle of excitement – Saturday night in the city, lights on, the illuminated old Customs gateway she loved near the Kaivalyadham. They inched their way towards Babulnath, and spent a while opposite Wilson College, talking, breathing in the exhaust emanations, and staring across the leafy road divider. From outside, the stone cloisters looked appealingly monastic. At Pedder Road, near the Hanging Gardens, another bottleneck. It went on like this.

'Man, the traffic is really bad,' Vikram said.

Leela looked at him.

'You can't go to a party on the train, Leela.'

At ten forty-five they got to Juhu and, about ten minutes later, to a large block-shaped house somewhere near the sea. The gate slid open. The watchman salaamed Vikram. Leela felt dazed, as though someone had said, 'Bombay? You like Bombay?' and then forced her to sit down and eat the entire city, spread out on a conveyor belt.

'How do you know Meena and Tara?' The sisters who were having the party.

'My parents used to know their parents.'

'Oh, so you've known them a long time?'

'Yeah, but mostly when we were kids. We used to have a beach house here, then we sold it when my father died. We met again a few years ago and hung out a few times when I was home from college. I guess that's when we really became friends. You'll like them.'

He paid the cab driver and they walked into the front door. A girl squealed, and jumped on Vikram. She was tiny, with long curly hair. 'Vik! I didn't know you'd be here. How *are* *you*?' She hung onto his arm, and leant into him, carried on talking. 'We're going to have so much fun tonight. Oh my God, I haven't seen you in sooo long. We have to hang out properly. Promise? Promise?' She was shaking her head and slapping his arm; Leela stood just inside the door.

'Excuse me.' A couple came in just after her.

'Oh, sorry.'

The man, a little shorter than Vikram, had a shaven head and bright, dark tadpole eyes. He wore a t-shirt and jeans. The girl with him was tall and slim. 'Come on Adi,' she said. He gave Leela a glance, of interest or snobbishness, she couldn't tell. Meanwhile the little girl in heels and her tiny dress was still clinging to Vikram.

'Shall we go inside?' Leela asked. She smiled at the girl, though by now she wanted to yelp.

'Good idea.' Vikram took her shoulder, and they walked in, the other girl behind them.

'Who's that?' Leela asked, but at this point he met another girl, who gave him a reproving but affectionate look and hugged him hard.

'Hi, I'm Tara,' she said.

'Hi, I'm Leela.'

Tara smiled.

Leela smiled. 'Um, so what do you do?' she asked.

Did the other girl's eyebrows rise slightly? 'I'm into interior decoration.'

'Oh, really?' Leela began a conversation about interior style, minimalism versus opulence, and only then noticed the house, which had obviously recently been reworked at some expense. In pauses of the conversation, Tara, who was smaller than she, slender, and fair, would smile sweetly. Leela felt her confidence drizzle away.

'Anyway, that must be amazing,' she said.

Tara smiled again.

Where the hell was Vikram? Leela saw him in a corner, still beset by the small, curly haired woman. As though suddenly, she noticed how well everyone was dressed. Some, like the tiny woman, wore cocktail dresses: hers was dark pink silk. Even Tara, who seemed to be casually dressed, wore a beautifully cut top, jeans, and heels, and her hair was impeccable. Leela tried not to stare at her own battered silver kolhapuris.

'You don't have a drink. What will you have?'

'Anything,' Leela said.

Tara beckoned a man in a white shirt and black trousers. 'Can you get her a drink?'

'Of course,' he said in perfect English. 'What would you like, ma'am?'

'Anything.'

'We have vodka, gin, tequila, single malt, beer, wine, champagne.'

'A glass of champagne?' Tara said.

'Sure.'

She touched Leela's arm. 'Can you excuse me for a minute? I need to welcome some guests.'

'Of course.' Leela moved out of the first room, and met the same waiter, if that's what he was, in the passage. He had a tray and delivered the glass of champagne to her.

'Thanks so much.'

She carried it, took a swig, and drifted out towards the open veranda and the garden. Maybe there was a corner here where she could sip her drink, sit behind a bush, and be quiet. The bush would inevitably be full of über-mosquitoes or something worse; another worryingly polite minion would appear and ask if she was all right.

She slunk onwards, rounded the veranda, and continued onto the lawn. Never mind getting back to Colaba by one. She was stuck.

Further out on the lawn there was no one. She walked up a rise and found a long pavilion that overlooked the beach. She remembered going there as a child. An uncle worked for a large company, and had borrowed the beach house of someone else in the company. They'd all gone for a few days – she and Neeti, her parents, and some cousins. Neeti, of course, had found a turd in the water and grabbed her, 'Look didi, look!' She'd wanted to take it back to show their mother; Leela had eventually dissuaded her. But this was another world. Tara, or the girl in the cocktail dress at whom Vikram smiled indulgently – it was unlikely they'd swum here as children. Perhaps they'd gone to the Cap d'Antibes? Or the Caribbean? She sat on the deck of the pavilion and took off her shoes. The grass was nice, damp and cool. It smelled of the beach: sea salt, something fetid, and a humid rise in the air.

She took another large glug of the champagne and began to feel buoyant. She should go back and find Vikram. She didn't want to. Duelling with another woman for a man's attention was an important female skill she'd never had – it seemed to involve things like confidence, hair flicking, talking loudly, touching the man in question, all techniques she'd memorised but never been able to implement. Instead, she went limp when she sensed such a contest had been thrown out, as though she couldn't bear to fail, but knew she would. She sat on the grass and felt a fictional euphoria – the warmth of the night, the glow of the party below, the champagne, a sense of being able to do anything, even march back into the house and vanquish the cocktail frock girl – without the burden of having to try.

The party and Vikram seemed far away, which felt pleasant. Her life, her parents' house, though intimate in a way this wasn't, also seemed removed, only provisionally hers. Even the hostel, though she thought now of her clean, slightly shabby cell with covetousness, was remote.

The sense of lightness gave her a pang of fear. She would go down, she determined, and find Vikram, find out how long they'd be here, what the plan was.

'Hello.'

It was the bald man from the door.

'Sorry,' said Leela viciously.

He sat down less than a yard from her. 'Why are you sorry?' He leant a bit closer. 'You're not a Brit, are you? You do have an accent.'

'No.'

'All right. I was just asking.' He had something white in his hand, and put it in his mouth. A scratch of flint, a flare, and it was lit. 'You don't mind about this?'

'No,' said Leela, much more nicely.

'Would you like to join me?'

'Mm. Maybe.'

'It really is very good. Someone brought it from Manali, or that's what I was told. For once it's …' and he paused to hold in the smoke. He exhaled. 'Ah.'

'For once it's?'

He stuck out his hand. 'I'm Aditya.'

'Leela.'

His hand was warm and, to her surprise, felt clean and unsuspect.

'Leela, Leela, Leela.' His voice was deep and pleasant. She wondered if he was going to irritate her, when he would pass over the joint, how long it'd take for her to get stoned, whether she'd be able to smoke properly, or if she'd have to take a couple of genteel puffs and pass it back. 'What are you thinking on this beautiful late summer night, in the open air?'

'I'm thinking when will you pass me the pétard,' said Leela.

'The what?'

'The joint.'

'What did you call it?'

'Pétard. It's slang. It's French.'

'Are you French?' He sat there, joint still in fingers. Leela waited.

'No.'

'Ah. Here. You seem to be a most fascinating person, Leela. Last name?'

'Ghosh.'

'A Bengali?'

'Not really.'

'Leela Ghosh, not really Bengali, knows French – fluently?' He cocked an eye at her.

'Not really.' She took a big hit and concentrated on puffing her chest out and not breathing.

'Not really fluently, alone in a hut thing in this beautiful garden, what are you doing here Leela Ghosh?'

She waited, puffed out like a night-time toad, reluctant to exhale.

'I think you may have absorbed the relevant toxins now, Miss Ghosh.'

She giggled and spluttered. 'Fuck.' And coughed. She looked at the joint and as a precautionary measure took another smaller hit before handing it back.

'You smoke very seriously. I don't think I've ever seen quite that expression before.'

'I'd hate to get it wrong.'

He was leaning back, his legs extended. He grinned.

Leela began to feel altered, as though the sensory world still existed, but she apprehended messages from it only after a gap of two or three seconds. He passed her the end of the joint. She extracted what she could, and kept the smoke in.

'So what are you doing here?' she asked.

'Tara, Meena, good friends of mine. Nice girls.'

'Do you know Vikram Sahni?'

'Vik, yeah, of course. You came with him?'

'Yeah.'

'Are you –'

'Am I –?'

Aditya chuckled. 'Chill out, Leela Ghosh. Otherwise I'm going to feel my good grass from Manali has been completely wasted on you.'

Leela laughed. 'This is a nice house, isn't it? Well, very large, beautiful – situation.'

'You mean having a house like this? I'd say.'

'That too, but I meant it's well situated, a nice piece of land, a great view.'

'Are you an estate agent?'

They both began to giggle.

Leela noticed Vikram striding up. He looked displeased, and grown up, his white shirt still impeccable. He is handsome, she thought, but boring. He looks like a cartoon of a handsome person. This thought made her, and in response her new friend, laugh even more.

'Hello Adi. What are you two up to?'

'Vik, come and sit down. Do you want some lovely grass? No, wait, we smoked it.'

'You're a charasi, that I know, but I didn't realise you were, Leela.' He looked down at her. She was starting to feel sick. At about this time Aditya began to seem superfluous. Below, the house was illuminated; it appeared quite far away. Leela tried to imagine standing up. Even thinking about it felt like a lot of effort.

'Ugh,' she said, without realising she'd spoken.

'Charming,' said Aditya.

Something occurred to Leela. 'What time is it?' she asked Vikram.

'Nearly one.'

'Oh.'

'Do you have a curfew?'

'Never mind.'

Aditya got up and lit a cigarette. 'Well, I'm going back down. See you later, Vik. It was nice talking to you, Leela Ghosh.'

They watched his swaying figure move towards the house. The night was warm and gentle. But Leela felt sick.

'Come on,' Vikram said. 'Or were you planning on sleeping here?' He put out a hand to her.

'What's your fucking problem?' She pushed away the hand and began to get up, though it seemed to take more marshalling of the limbs than she'd realised. Her legs bounded around like an uncoordinated frog. 'Ah.' She stood. I have done something stupid to my body, she thought, with the old sadness. Things weren't bad, but I misunderstood them, and created a bad situation.

'It's all so needless,' she said.

'What?' He looked angry.

'Doesn't matter.'

'I was looking for you, you know. I thought we'd come together to the party. You were talking to Tara, then you weren't there, and I looked around for you and had no idea where you were. I called your phone six times.'

'You were talking to that girl anyway.'

'Which girl?'

'Oh, bullshit. Fucking bullshit.'

They began to make their way, stumblingly in Leela's case, down the hill. Vikram grabbed her wrist.

'Ow!' she said. The resentment in her voice made her aware she was angry.

'Okay, walk by yourself. Do you mean Niharika?'

'That girl in the pink dress who wouldn't stop staring at you and chirruping.'

'She's a friend's younger sister. I've known her a long time.'

'You didn't even introduce me. It was like you totally forgot I was there.'

'I introduced you to Tara.'

'But then you ignored me.'

'Don't be crazy, Leela.'

They were at the foot of the small slope, nearing the main garden.

'Fuck off,' said Leela, raising the ante slightly more than she'd intended.

He paused mid-stride. 'What?'

'Just stop being horrible to me. Leave me alone. You're the one who ignored me.'

He came to a complete standstill. They were outside the lit veranda, and Leela had a thought, half paranoid, half interested, that someone might hear.

He looked at her, his face again not easy to read. 'How do you think you'd get home?'

'I'd manage.'

'Well, I'm not going to leave a girl in a part of town she doesn't know in the middle of the night, sorry.'

They walked through the party, and Vikram got caught near the door to say goodbye to the sisters. 'Don't go!' cried the younger, Meena.

He grinned. 'I have to get Leela back.'

She regarded Leela with comic hostility. 'Stay. Aren't you having a good time?'

'I'm having such a good time,' Leela said. 'I just have to go, I live in a hostel.'

Meena's face was baffled. 'So go tomorrow. Vik, do something.'

'We have to go. Thanks for a great evening.'

Tara said, 'Let them go, Meenu. They've had enough of you.'

'You bitch.' She pinched her sister in mock rage.

They finally escaped. The night outside was weirdly normal, a man selling cigarettes down the lane. At the end of it, a rickshawala with whom Vikram negotiated to take them to Bandra. The sea road, then the highway, frightening and anonymous: along it, construction sites and makeshift shelters of tarpaulin, thin men and women around a fire; long stretches of slums. She couldn't orient herself, and was silently glad not to be alone. She leaned forward onto her knees, wondered if she would be sick, felt tired.

Vikram took her shoulder, and made her lean back.

At Bandra, near the station, they got into a taxi.

Leela leant back in the seat as more familiar parts of town, like Cadell Road, passed.

They were outside the Buddhist temple at Worli when he said, 'So why were you so angry?'

The roads were nearly empty, just a few drunken drivers and the odd taxi. She said, 'I don't know. I felt self-conscious, I didn't know anyone, I didn't know what to expect.'

'I was only being friendly to Niharika, I've known her forever.'

'Good for you.'

He grabbed her wrist. 'What's going on?'

I'm going to be sick, Leela thought.

'I'm crazy about you, Leela.'

It registered on her that they were on Annie Besant Road, passing the high walls of the GlaxoSmithKline compound, popularly referred to as 'Glasgow'.

'So am I,' she managed, her heart dully thumping in the conviction of imminent calamity.

Just before the flyover, Vikram's face loomed closer to hers, his expression tender, and briefly she caught the taxi driver's eye in the mirror, cynical, interested.

28

His hand was on the curve of her waist; the top of her right foot rested warm in his left instep. They lay there for a while.

'Why?' she asked.

He sighed, an exhalation she felt as well as hearing: a warm snuffle, a heave of the chest.

'She'll just immediately get into gear. She'll want to know how serious it is.'

She went tense. 'How serious is it?'

His arm tightened about her. He was always willing to be demonstrative. 'It's serious.'

'I feel like it's weird, this being shifty around her. Why?'

He sighed again. Leela looked at the white-painted corner of his bedside table with something like recognition. The furniture in his room had come to seem intimate with her.

Her days were Vikram interleaved with things that were not Vikram: work, the increasingly unreal life of the hostel, which now served as a place where she returned late, tired, and crashed out, or woke in a brief lull, disoriented, and then recalled what she had to do in the day. Which was, to rise, to meditate in a token way, though all she did now was to feel excited, almost ill with a rash of thoughts, and then to bathe, wash her clothes, pack her bag, and go to work again.

'Where *are* you these days?' asked Chitra, bumping into her in the porch.

Leela grinned.

'Aha! I knew it. Shobha saw you going out to meet some guy. Is it the same one? Come to my room.'

They went up. Leela enjoyed the urgency that seemed to attach to her. She told her story; earlier, she'd mentioned Vikram to Chitra, but diffidently.

'So you like him now?'

'Of course. I really like him.' She thought it an annoying question. She was sitting on the floor; she leaned back onto her hands.

'I'm really pleased for you,' Chitra said. She looked awkward.

This is what it'll be like, Leela thought. People will be envious, they won't know what to say. She said what Amy might have said. 'Well, who knows if it'll work out.' Immediately she regretted her tone.

Chitra looked surprised. 'I'm sure it will,' she said quietly. Leela was aware of being consoled and felt irritated. 'It sounds great,' Chitra said. 'I think he really likes you.' She continued to look at Leela speculatively.

'Are you going to dinner?'

'Come.'

She waited at work to tell Sathya, who didn't show up the next day.

'Hey, coming for a cigarette?' she asked as soon as she walked in and saw him.

'Ten minutes.'

She waited. When they went outside and he lit up, she said, 'So remember the guy I was talking about, Vikram?'

'Your friend?'

'We got together.'

'Oh, really?' Sathya was looking a bit ashen. 'Hey, good for you.'

'It turns out he did like me.'

'Of course he did,' he said absently.

Leela gave up.

She didn't go home for a fortnight, but one Saturday Vikram had a wedding to go to.

'Are you going to tell your mother?' Leela asked.

'I'll tell her,' he said finally.

She went home for the weekend.

On Monday Sathya wasn't in office. She had to remind herself of the constructions she used to use, and those she'd adopted in order not to sound different: the later ones had come to have their own rightness, like *in office* for *in the office*. She tried to archive the earlier usage so she wouldn't forget it, the purity of Standard English reinforced by school books. She was always having to learn things that would enable her to fit in, but those lessons were always being replaced.

She worked hard, finished the mailing for a trustees' dinner, called the secretaries of each trustee to confirm dietary preferences and spent two hours waiting to get the seating plan approved before Joan trashed it and said impatiently, 'I'll explain tomorrow.'

It was annoying that Sathya wasn't there. Leela wanted to talk to someone, begin to delineate her vague unease.

But Vikram, reliably, was there. She would meet him as soon as she'd been home and changed and dropped off her things. And when she was in the hostel, with its hive-like chatter in the evening, the tube lights in the reception area flickering on and thrumming, and the girls either arriving in work clothes, handbags held officiously, hair half up; or floating around, lax, in printed wrappers that may have resembled what their mothers wore at home to be comfortable, she found herself exhausted, not wanting to leave the bustle of the hive, where she could be quiet.

When she arrived to meet Vikram, some minutes late, as she'd begun to be, he was radiant. He gave her a hug. 'I missed you, baby.'

'I missed you too. What happened?'

He grinned hugely. 'You're coming over for dinner on Saturday. Mummy wants to meet you.'

On Saturday morning she had a dream about Roger. They were hugging tenderly. He smelled the same: vaguely alkaline, vaguely lemony, but underneath of musk. His shirt was soft at her cheekbone. He wanted to persist in the hug, and the dreaming Leela was aware of how comforting it was: she wanted to remain in it too. The Leela in the dream, though, broke away. 'Why?' she asked. 'Why? Why?' She was inconsolable and in this moment Leela awoke. She felt terrible sadness, the conviction she'd done the wrong thing, and the usual despair at her own weak will, the lack of control or decisiveness in her subconscious. What a stupid dream, she thought, and lay still and sorrowful, regretting that it was over.

'Lovely to see you, Leela,' Vikram's mother said.

'It's lovely to see you too,' Leela said. She began to step out of her chappals, and Shalini raised an eyebrow. 'You don't need to take off your shoes, dear.'

'It's just that I walk everywhere,' Leela said.

'Keep them on, we all do.' Did Vikram's mother look down at her feet briefly? Leela followed her into the drawing room. Even when she had spent time in the flat, in the afternoon or early evening when Shalini had been out, she and Vikram hadn't been in here. Now, she felt she was transgressing. Vikram's mother must have realised they had been in the flat; the servant had probably told her.

Shalini turned and smiled at Leela, who saw incisors. She bumped into the corner of a sideboard and said, 'Oh, sorry.'

'What would you like to drink?'

'I –' She looked around for Vikram.

Shalini, elegant, collected, watched her. 'There's gin, whisky, vodka. Rum, I think. Or a glass of wine?'

'Sure.'

'Which one, dear?'

'Is there any wine open?'

'Would you like red or white?'

'White, please.' Leela went red. Was this a test?

'I'll get a bottle opened. Gopal?'

The servant, clad in white, appeared. He was thin and in manner elliptical, at least when Leela had seen him; often, when she had been in the flat at quieter times, he had been out or in his tiny room at the end of the kitchen, the radio distantly audible. He said, 'Madam?'

'White wine laana. Naya bottle. Jo fridge mein hai.'

He nodded and went away.

'Let's sit,' Shalini said.

They sat on perpendicular sides of a corner sofa. Leela realised that she hated this room, and why; it had been ordered for display, to convey massiveness and money. She could not imagine anyone sinking onto the sofa to read delightedly, or stare at a wall and think.

Gopal came back with a tray, a chilled bottle of wine, and two glasses.

'Madam ko dena,' Shalini said. Leela got a glass of wine.

'What about you?' she asked.

'Oh, I don't really drink,' Shalini said. She smiled. Ah, thought Leela. I drink copiously, she imagined saying. Don't you find it smoothes out every social occasion? She took a sip of the wine. It was medium-dry, pleasant.

'How is the wine?'

'Lovely, thank you.' When would Vikram emerge?

'Good. We got some new bottles. It's French, I think. I haven't tasted it.'

'It's very nice.' Leela took another sip. She imagined saying something in the manner of the blonde, bobbed woman from a wine programme on TV in her youth. 'Acidic, fresh, just a *whiff* of cat's pee.'

Shalini smiled. 'So you live in the hostel, Vikram tells me? The one near Sassoon Dock?'

'Near the Post Office, yes.'

'How do you find that? Do you have a lot of friends there?'

'A few. It takes time, of course. But I have some really nice friends here now.'

'Ah yes, you used to be in England, is that right?'

'I grew up there, mostly, but I'm from Bombay.'

'But your parents don't live in Bombay?'

'No, they're in Pune.'

'That must be very pleasant. I believe the weather there is very good? I haven't been for years. Since it was Poona.' Shalini spoke so calmly, in such a measured way, and Leela admired her poise. Everything was where it ought to be, her short silver hair blow-dried, her earrings impeccable, her silk shirt beautifully pressed; there wasn't the sense of a frenetic attempt to keep things under control that was there in Leela's mother. But, she thought, none of the fire either.

Shalini's fine eyes examined her. 'And how do you like being an independent woman in Bombay?'

Leela tried to discern whether there was sarcasm in the question; she didn't think so. 'I like it. I love the city, I always have.'

'Bombay can be a difficult place for a woman on her own.'

'I like it,' Leela persisted. She looked at her feet. Her worn kolhapuris were in a white plush rug.

'You have a very simple look, very nice,' Shalini said. 'Where do you go for your services, which parlour?'

Leela blinked.

'Your pedicure, waxing, things like that?' The other woman's eyes lingered on Leela's arms, which weren't waxed.

'Oh, I don't. I've never really –'

Again, the fine kohl-lined eyes considered her. 'Touch of Joy,' said Shalini gently, 'at BEST Marg, it's really very good. If you're in a hurry, they have two girls waxing at the same time.'

Leela was baffled.

'You know, so you save time.'

She nodded.

'And of course, you must come here for a meal any time. Consider it your home,' Shalini added much more warmly, and Leela was confused. She must be misjudging this; she both admired and disliked this woman and couldn't understand why. The conversation had moved away from the form she had anticipated, but it had now again become recognisable; perhaps she had simply, through stupidity, failed to give the proper responses and that was why it had departed from its theme before returning, like a song, to the melody.

Vikram was in the room, he bent and kissed his mother. Then Leela. 'Hi,' he said. He smelled fresh, had evidently just bathed.

'Hi,' she said, understanding now.

She didn't get a chance to discuss it with Vikram, for she didn't see him for two days. Chitra was out of town. She wondered, she rehearsed conversations in her head. I like her, she began, but she makes me feel unsure. There's something;

I can't tell what she really feels about anything. People are weird about their sons. Mothers.

'It went really well, didn't it?' Vikram said with joy on Tuesday.

'Yes, of course,' Leela said. She wondered that he couldn't tell.

'Mummy said you seem like a lovely person.'

'She did?'

'Of course. What did you think she'd say?'

Smart woman, thought Leela glumly.

'I like your mother,' she said later. 'I just think she has more interest in whether or not I get a pedicure than whether I speak French or have a degree.' When she named these accomplishments, they sounded equally irrelevant to her.

'She knows you care about me, and that's what matters,' Vikram said. He looked surprised, and when it dawned on him, hurt. 'Do you think you're giving her credit? It can't be easy to feel relaxed when you meet your son's girlfriend. It's not a concept she's had a lot of experience of in real life.'

'What did she say?' Leela asked. Her vanity was curious, but more than that she burned to understand the unnamed, not-quite-personal hostility under the flawless manners.

'She asked me if we're going to get married,' he said.

'Oh. What did you say?'

'I said I hope so.' His hug was quick.

'Oh!' There was nowhere for her affront, so ready to appear, to go.

237

'I feel,' said Chitra, folding a pile of clean but unironed clothes, 'that you talk more about Vikram's mother than about Vikram.'

Leela was annoyed, and laughed. 'Maybe she's a worthier adversary.'

They both laughed.

'No, it's not that,' she said, ashamed of herself. 'I can't tell what she's thinking. I nearly said, I can't tell what she's up to.'

On the balcony outside, pigeons made soft, iterative noises: Oooo-oo, ooo-oo.

I will leave here at some point, if Vikram and I do marry, this phase of my life will have ended, Leela thought, looking at the white formica-topped desk and the steel cupboard. I will not be stuck here, or like those girls you see at dinner who talk about looking for a place to live because their term is nearly over: paying-guest accommodation in Colaba or Warden Road, or a shared flat in Bandra or further out: Andheri, Borivali, Navi Mumbai.

She caught Chitra looking at her.

'I feel like there's an unspoken thing going on between me and her that she thinks I understand. But I don't. I can tell there's some sort of battle taking place though.'

'What d'you expect? She's a widow, only son, obviously she's paranoid. You could marry him and then treat her really badly.'

'Like an aunt of my father's,' Leela remembered. 'Her daughter-in-law even kept the sugar locked up and didn't give her a key. When my father went to see her she couldn't make him a cup of tea. I'd never do anything like that.'

Chitra wrapped her unironed clothes in an old sheet and tied the ends in a knot.

'Let's go down,' she said. 'I'm hungry and I want to catch the dhobi.'

'Why does everyone call him the dhobi when most people just give him their clothes for istri?' enquired Leela as they got into the lift.

Chitra laughed, as people tended to when Leela asked linguistic questions. 'Because he will also wash clothes, I suppose. I don't know.'

I am right only about useless things, Leela thought.

'I thought of bringing a friend to lunch on Saturday,' she told her father on the telephone, knowing he wouldn't say no.

'A friend?'

'My friend Vikram, er, actually my boyfriend.'

There was a pause. 'Lovely, yes. What does he eat or not eat?' Mr Ghosh enquired. Leela cringed, imagining his expression at the other end of the line, the look of warning or having something to elaborate on that he might have given her mother.

'Everything, he eats everything. Don't worry too much about the food,' she said.

So it happened that Vikram was sitting in her parents' drawing room, on the sofa, where a jittery Leela also sat. He reached for her hand; she tried hard not to see her parents not rolling their eyes at each other. Every time Vikram spoke she was aware of unbelievably convoluted pathways and tables of rules in the air which only she – and perhaps Neeti, had she cared – could perceive. She found it impossible not to notice them.

'So what do you do, Vikram?' her mother was asking. Vikram had a cold beer next to him.

'Well, I'm still looking around, auntie,' he said. 'But I have a master's in international relations, so I'm interested in working in policy development.'

'What does that mean, concretely?'

Without wanting to, Leela found herself, while the interrogation was taking place, seeing it all through her parents' eyes, and detaching herself inwardly from Vikram. Or was it that her own thoughts, which she'd suppressed in her pleasure at being loved, were now arising again?

'Working for a policy shaping organisation, for example. Attending meetings, local government.'

Leela's father chuckled. 'You'd find that pretty tedious, I think.'

'Baba,' said Leela.

'No, you're right. But some of us have to get involved. Otherwise all the resources of this country seep away into low-level corruption, and we wonder at dinner parties why nothing works and so many people are still poor.'

Leela was afresh impressed by, and mildly irritated with, Vikram.

When her father was driving her to the station on Sunday he said, 'Nice fellow. Seems very nice. Seems quite young.'

'He's a year older than me.'

'Ah? Maybe he just needs to find out what he wants to do in life. Business family, you said?'

'He knows what he wants to do.'

They had rounded the station road, and were waiting to turn into the chaotic parking lot.

'You're pretty serious?' Her father sounded mildly regretful, but that was a habit.

'Yes,' Leela said firmly.

She spent the journey staring, melancholic, out of the yellow-tinted windows of the chair car. When Bombay and its filth approached – miles of slums and rubbish on the tracks, people harvesting greens grown near them, and industrial chimneys pumping clouds of smoke into a pearly, polluted sky – her heart didn't flip, as usual, with happiness. She sighed, ready to re-enter her world, and at VT hurried into the dark station, where shadows moved like former people along the night-time platform.

29

'Hold on. Mummy wants to talk to you. I think about lunch.'

Leela was left mouthing 'What?' to herself in the mirror after the fashion of a cartoon character. She looked at her reflection: were Tintinesque drops of perspiration flying from her face in alarm?

'Hello?'

A pause. Vikram's mother was the kind of woman who managed to be ineffably feminine even on the telephone. 'Hello?' she said softly.

Oh come on, thought Leela. 'Hi, Mrs Sahni.'

'Shalini, Leela.'

'Hello Shalini.'

Pause.

'Leela, I was wondering if you might have the time to have lunch with me one day?'

'Oh. That's very kind.'

'Will it be possible for you? This week?'

'Well …'

'Which day?'

'Thursday?' It was far enough off, she could tell Joan a couple of days before.

'Lovely. One o'clock?'

'One o'clock.'

'See you then, my dear.'

Leela remained looking at the phone. Shalini had hung up.

On Tuesday she forgot to chase the istriwala for her iron-ing; on Wednesday she was late home and missed him. She couldn't wear her smarter clothes, therefore. She took out various things from the closet, examined them, wondered where she and Shalini might go for lunch, tried to imagine what her motives were – perhaps just a simple thought of eating lunch together, or feeding the hostelite Leela. Had it been one of those lunches, the sort her mother would take her to when she was in Bombay for work, clothes would have been tertiary. The main focus would have been large quanti-ties of good food. Swati Snacks, for example, or Vithal Bhelwala, or Samovar. Back to the lunch at hand, she couldn't work out what Vikram's mother wanted, if anything. Anyway, she couldn't go suspiciously dressed up, even had this been possible, to the office. Questions would be asked. Sathya – who seemed to be looking more and more haggard, and was out of the office as much as once a week – would notice, ask what was up. Joan would enjoy keeping Leela on a random pretext.

She put on an embroidered sleeveless top that her mother said was nice, and a pair of jeans and forgot about it except for the need to keep an eye on the time all morning lest she be late to meet Shalini outside Regal. As the last half-hour in the office approached she began to feel strange. Sathya wasn't there. Joan raised an eyebrow but said nothing as Leela went to the loo three times in thirty minutes to check her hair.

'I'll go now, for my lunch.'

Joan nodded.

Leela bolted. She couldn't get a cab to go the short distance but had left herself just enough time to walk. Her heart raced, she wondered if she would be late, or smell sweaty and look dishevelled. Car and truck exhausts seemed to want to breathe on her; the April heat was intense; she nearly had her foot run over twice by an amorous motorcyclist. She got to Regal and tried not to look panicked. Her face must be shiny. Breathe. She squinted into the glare.

A thin young man came up.

'Hello madam, how are you?' he asked in polite Bombay Hindi.

He looked young and was neatly dressed in shirt-pant. Leela smiled at him and looked away.

'Madam, do you want a map? World map hai, India map hai.' He opened the A2 posters and began to unfurl them.

'No, thanks.'

The sun glinted off the lamination. She felt a childish attraction to them, perhaps because they resembled the comic books she'd loved in childhood, or perhaps because of the large expanses of turquoise sea. Her knowledge of the different states and some of the smaller cities was poor; she began to peer at Andhra Pradesh.

'Le lo Madam, le lo. Main aaj hi aaya hun Bambai,' he began to whine. Buy one, I only came to Bombay today, 'yeh mera pehla din hai, le lo', this is my first day, please buy one. 'Bahut achcha hoga aap ke liye', it'll bring you luck.

'You're saying it won't be lucky for you? How much are they?'

'Two hundred rupees.'

'No way.'

'Please madam, it's my first day, no one's bought one, please, it'll be very good for you, take one, take two, I'll give you a good price.'

What if it really was his first day in the city? She remembered sitting in the café here on a Saturday morning, reading the newspaper, ignoring the white tourists, watching the street kids eye them through the glass.

'I'll give you a hundred rupees.'

'No madam, very good quality, special price for you, one-fifty.'

'Okay.' She chose a map of India, political, with many place names in each state, and the seas clearly marked: Indian Ocean, Bay of Bengal, Arabian Sea. There was Kanyakumari at the tip. She felt the same strong but obscure patriotism that she recalled from childhood, watching the Republic Day parade on a neighbour's television. Those memories were concrete but seemed fictional; not more fictional, though, than London, or Richard, or school and its unending misery.

She gave him the money and he rolled the map up for her and produced a rubber band to hold it in place. Leela stood looking at it. A minute later, he came up behind her again.

'Madam?'

She wheeled around, snapping, 'I just bought one, didn't I?'

It was Shalini's driver.

'Madam is waiting,' he said.

'Coming.'

The car was parked in a side road, and Leela, holding the map, got in.

'Hi,' she said.

'Hello dear. I was worried you were lost.'

'No, I was there, I just – I got caught up. This boy was selling these.'

The car had started moving again, the air conditioning was on.

Leela tried to wedge the rolled-up map into a less inconvenient place near her leg. Vikram's mother wore white slacks, perfectly pressed, and a sort of kurta blouse. She carried a tan handbag.

'He said it was his first day in Bombay,' Leela said.

'Oh yes, they always say things like that.'

'No, I really think it might have been.'

'I don't think so, dear.'

Leela opened her mouth to argue and shut it again. They rolled up at the Taj.

'I thought we might go to Souk, they have a nice lunch buffet,' Shalini said.

'Great.' Leela wasn't sure whether to leave the poster in the car. A large turbaned man was holding open the door. She got out, still holding the map.

'Perhaps we can have a look at the shops later,' Shalini said, as they crossed the lobby.

'Yes, sure.' Leela was both rebellious and embarrassed in the perennial scruffy kolhapuris and jeans, amid the brocade furniture and smiling staff. 'I like the Taj best of all the hotels in Bombay,' she told Shalini. 'I like the pretty girls who open the door for you and smile and say hello. Sometimes it's nice just to come here for the air conditioning and the loo and the smile.'

She was confiding, but Vikram's mother raised an eyebrow and remained silent.

Leela tried to continue talking while they were led to a table near the enormous windows.

'The view is lovely,' she said, as a waiter served hot starters and tripped over the rolled-up map under her chair.

The view was lovely: Bombay, grey, hazy, slightly diminished through tinted glass; the sea, and a small island which the navy used.

Shalini smiled.

Leela worked her way through humous, tahini, and aubergine dip, and wondered why she wasn't enjoying the food more. It was the Taj, after all. When she had to come here for a meeting she fell on the biscuits and tea with delight. Now, she wasn't having a particularly good time. The food was also boring. You could eat dirtier, tastier versions of the same thing off the Edgware Road.

'Are you enjoying the food?'

'Yes, delicious,' she said, obliged to eat more pitta bread.

'My dear, I notice you don't – you don't wear very much jewellery. You dress very simply, which is nice. But I wondered if you've seen some of the newer designers at boutiques like the Courtyard? You might really like them.'

Leela nodded.

'You girls today have so much to do, and that's wonderful. So many opportunities. But it's also important to be presentable, take care of that side of things.'

Leela smiled.

'Maybe it would be nice if you got a manicure once a month or so. And you might not know, you haven't lived in Bombay long, I can point out the best dry-cleaner. There is a place in Colaba, but the best thing is to save a few pieces and send them to Beauty Art at Churchgate.'

'Right.'

'I have a good fellow who makes sari blouses, too, for when you need to go to a formal occasion. You have some saris?'

'I generally wear my mother's. She has some old temple saris and Bengali silks. But I don't really know how to tie a sari.'

Vikram's mother seemed exhilarated. 'It's just a case of working with what you have,' she whispered. 'Do you see?'

Leela didn't, and nodded. She wondered if she should claim to be going to the loo and leave. What would happen? She couldn't do that. She thought of Vikram's delighted face. 'Mummy wants to spend some time with you.'

You can't suppose, Leela said silently, that I will do what you want. I don't even do what my parents want, as a point of principle, and I care about them.

'You know, there is an adjustment, when you're with someone, and with their family and friends. It's a new start, in many ways. But it can be fun.'

'Mm.'

'When I got married, I was much younger than you. Those were different times. I'd just finished college. Vikram was born a year later. I had to learn in a hurry. There are some mistakes it isn't worth making for yourself.'

Leela nodded. She was unsure what was being talked about. Birth control?

'Any dessert for you, dear?'

'No thanks, I'm really full,' Leela said, then felt despondent, remembering the expression was inelegant. What were you supposed to say? 'I'm satisfied', or something of the sort. 'I couldn't possibly', but that might be as vulgar as sticking your little finger out when drinking tea. She grinned. Vikram's mother gave her an odd look.

In the arcade downstairs they stopped outside a jeweller's. 'Do you see those earrings? Very lovely. And quite simple, really.' Shalini pointed at a pair of enamelled chandelier earrings, set with uncut diamonds.

'Yes, beautiful.'

'We should come back here. First maybe shoes.'

In the shoe shop, Shalini pointed out with approval various styles. 'Those look smart, don't you think?' Elegant tan shoes.

'Yes.'

'Or those.' Jewelled wedges. Those look Sindhi, thought Leela, reprising her sister's summary of some cousins' sequinned clothing and footwear.

'Maybe a bit bling for me.'

'They also make kolhapuris. Would you like to see? Very elegant.'

'I'm wearing kolhapuris.' Leela smiled.

Shalini asked the salesmen, who brought out silver and coloured kolhapuris with and without heels, their soles stamped with the shop's logo.

'They're nice. But a lot more expensive than the ones I get in Pune, and those are from Kolhapur,' Leela said.

Shalini's face became blank. 'Maybe we can look in the jeweller's again.'

Over trays of velvet and across from the wily face of a polite man with a moustache, Leela allowed herself to be bought a pendant and chain. The pendant was silver, meena-kari work with glass rather than diamonds in the back. The enamelling was delicate; it was crescent shaped, larger than things she normally wore.

'It's very pretty, thank you so much,' she said.

'It's only silver, but I think it's a good idea to start wearing some jewellery.'

'I normally avoid buying or being given things that I might be sorry if I lost when I move,' Leela said.

A hand fell lightly on her shoulder. 'Well, you're settled now. So you can stop doing that.'

Leela was startled, as though some deeper part of her consciousness had been disturbed; as though someone had interfered with her back. 'Yes.'

A few evenings later, alone at the hostel, she tried to sort through the various pieces of information and impressions in her mind. Shalini's face, slightly sharp, waiting, and her words, which seemed innocuous and yet which Leela couldn't quite understand; then Vikram, who wanted to see her every day, to talk on the phone when he got home from dropping her off, who was always slightly early when she had to meet him; then her increasing sense of disorientation. She had lost direction, and was moving away from everything that was familiar. There were too many things to get in order. When she tried, they slid around, and would not stay. Sitting on her bed, trying to think, for she was sure that if she could think about it with concentration and calm, it would all make sense, she missed dinner. She undressed, got into bed, and fell deeply asleep. In the night she woke, hungry and tired, and didn't manage to get up to drink water; the cooler was two floors away.

She dreamt of Richard. She was standing naked in front of his closet with him before they got ready. He knew about Vikram; he was saying to her, 'It won't work out. You're not over me yet.'

Her heart flipped in terror, as though she would be found out. He opened the closet and from the top shelf took a bowler hat.

'See?' he said.

She wore the hat, then tried to hide it in her room, but it kept falling out of the cupboard or sliding out from under the bed. Vikram was there. His face was disappointed.

'It's not my fault!' she cried.

In the morning she had a fever. She asked the bai not to clean, and slept till the afternoon. She couldn't see Vikram, and he called and became more worried. The next afternoon he came to pick her up. She had packed a few clothes; he was taking her to his house.

When in the hostel, sweating into her sheet, she had worried about nothing, simply following each exhausting stage of the fever: dreaming she was walking down a long, dilapidated corridor to look for someone, with someone else chasing her; when she arrived the person she was looking for wasn't there, and she left again. Her only fear was of the hostel rule that when residents became unwell they must be taken to their local guardian's home. Leela's LG was a cousin of her mother, elderly, living in Bandra; she didn't relish the idea of phoning her.

'But what about your mother?' she said to Vikram in the taxi. The outside world was bright, there was too much of it. She felt weaker, though she had been in bed for just two nights and a day.

'Well, you know her. Of course she didn't want you to stay alone while you were ill.'

She was too tired to resist, and beginning to feel lonely from the inevitability of the fever. She worried about dying, or suffering a relapse of the jaundice; inside, she had a sense that she must not damage herself. In the future, no matter how bad things appeared now, there would be things she must do.

Vikram took her to the spare room, where the blinds were already drawn, the air conditioner on.

'Can you turn the AC off?' she asked.

She got into bed, under a thick blanket lined with a sheet.

'Let me get some limbu paani. Gopal!'

'I don't want,' said Leela, and fell back into the long, slow funnel of her fever.

In the hours that appeared afterwards, Vikram was her friend. She would wake and find herself, wondering, in the spare room which came to imprint itself in her mind as one of the spaces where she had existed. Vikram would often be there too, reading in a chair near the bed or typing on his laptop. He came to lie in bed with her, and put his arms around her, his face in her hair. 'I love you, Leela,' he said.

They hadn't yet had sex. Between Leela's lunch of soup and an afternoon nap, they did. It was over soon. Feeling feverish, she held him and lay in his arms. The afternoon continued to unfold. She thought of the servant going out to shop and coming home to start the cooking, an endless routine of tasks after making lunch and cleaning in the morning. Her grandparents had also had a live-in servant, but Gopal was required to wear a white uniform. He called Vikram's mother madam, rather than memsahib; Leela supposed this was considered more modern or westernised or something.

Lying in bed with her that afternoon, Vikram told her about his childhood. At eight, when his parents' marriage was breaking down, he had been sent to boarding school near Panchgani. He'd known something was going on, but not what; he had been so lonely and miserable that he hadn't been able to focus on what was happening at home. His father had been having an affair with a married woman, a family friend; it had looked serious. In the end, he stayed, but five years later he died of a heart attack.

'Mummy had a really difficult time,' he said. Leela, facing away from him, made sympathetic noises. She began to understand some of the other woman's rage.

'Has she been interested in anyone else since then?'

Vikram's hand tightened on her hip; he swallowed. 'I think there was something with a friend of ours, who's divorced, when I was in England. I think. But I think she ended it.'

'You know him?' She turned to him.

He nodded.

'They didn't want to get married or anything?'

'I don't know. I don't know if she'd marry again. Or maybe he didn't want to.'

'How did you know they were seeing each other?'

'I still don't know for sure. His daughter said something to me. And once or twice, when I was here in the holidays I thought I heard his voice early in the morning, when I was sleeping, but Mummy said no one had come home.'

In the evening, when Leela was half asleep, she dreamt of a Christmas at Amy's, the electric blankets Amy's mother had put into their beds so that the sheets were warm when they came back from town at night ... How hot she was. She sweated and turned. But it wasn't she who'd taken part in these things, she knew that, and she was bewildered at the wealth of happenings that were attached to the surface of her experience. She woke to find a young man, bearded, grave, sitting at the side of the bed. She was definitely supposed to know him; for a minute she couldn't remember his name. Vikas, she thought. No.

His face lit up, and she was embarrassed. 'I came to bring you something. Do you want to get up for dinner?'

She sat up. 'No. No. I might have a bath.' She began to shiver. 'Or tomorrow.'

'Do you want some soup? Juice? Mummy's asking. She said you should eat.'

Something in Leela recoiled.

'Nothing?'

A sense came to her, more than an image, of the quiet corridor to her bedroom at her parents' flat, and birds singing outside in the afternoon.

'I want to go home,' she said, and to her surprise heard in her voice a sound of crying.

30

She padded down the corridor, unheeding, towards the dining table. Her father, from one of the cane chairs: 'You remember you had to call Vikram back?'

Leela slowed down, forgot what she had wanted in the kitchen, came out holding a glass of water. 'I'll call him,' she said.

She went back to her room. She was about to have a bath, she was in the state of being about to have a bath, she was sitting on the armchair and listening to birds outside: babblers. They sounded like Donald Ducks quacking at each other, cartoonish, comically disoriented.

She looked at the slim book on her bed, picked it up, read a few lines. She put it down, and stretched out her legs. She would have a bath, perhaps even do a few sun salutations, some stretches. She would meditate. She imagined herself doing so. The sun meanwhile came in from the balcony door and left a hot strip on the tiles. She put her foot in it, and the skin became more alive. She closed her eyes, and remembered yesterday and the journey back from Bombay.

'We should just get married, you know,' Vikram had said. He'd smiled at her. They had been in the taxi, driving her back, and about to pull into a service station so that the driver could have tea and a cigarette, and Leela go to the bathroom.

'Huh?' She had been pleased he was willing to say it, but warier than she had expected to be.

'I could marry you tomorrow, you know. I don't have any doubts.'

'I could marry you tomorrow, too,' she'd said. They'd discussed it earlier, in the days of their friendship: the need to reach a certain phase in one's life, to become a householder, to enter the world and leave behind the selfish days of youth. To establish oneself, to decide things, so that everything else, life, could take place. She'd agreed that it was what she needed, stability. She went shakily off to the bathroom and peed squatting in the Indian-style loo. She watched and smelt her own pee, pee-smelling, come out and go down into the not-overly-clean ceramic basin. At the sink, she washed her hands with someone else's leftover paper soap; she never remembered to carry it. The toilets smelt of phenyl. Outside, the service station smelt of petrol and frying and men's piss and cigarettes and tea. All these things were real. She tried to imagine her future life as another real thing among them, Vikram her husband, waiting for her in the car, in the sun outside.

She didn't call him back; in the afternoon he had to call again. For the whole of that week and half of the next she didn't go to work. She called Joan to say she had a stomach bug, which was vague but serious enough to be indisputable. When she did go back to Bombay, determined as a ghost returning to the scene of the crime, she handed in a note at the hostel saying that she was leaving, and giving a month's notice per the terms of her contract. She handed a similar letter, typed, to Joan, saying she had valued her time at the charity and thanking Joan for her kindness. Sathya was not in the office. His mother was dying of a late-discovered cancer that had metastised.

'I didn't know,' Leela said.

'I thought y'all were such good friends, I'm surprised he didn't tell you,' Joan said.

Over the next month, Leela saw Vikram several times. They met in the park near the hostel, and talked into the evening. Sometimes they sat on a bench that looked onto the shore, where, in the morning, you saw people who lived in the nearby slums shitting, then washing themselves. Sometimes they sat atop an artificial hillock in the centre of the park; when a girl Leela knew by sight from the hostel passed, she would cringe, then think, What does it matter?

Vikram cried. He said he'd never love anyone else. 'That's it,' he said. 'I'll be single now. There's no point being with someone else. It wouldn't mean anything.'

'You'll get married before I do,' Leela said.

Chitra helped her pack her things the day before her mother came to pick her up. 'Better than going through with an engagement, then calling it off,' she said.

'Did you think this would happen?' Leela asked. She couldn't bear to think of her failures as signal to all the world but herself.

'Do you want these newspapers? You can give them to the bai to sell if not.'

'No.'

'I wondered if you'd get bored with him,' the other girl admitted.

'What if it was time to settle down, what if this is the wrong thing to do?'

'Nothing is irreversible. You could tell him you've changed your mind now, if you wanted.'

Leela stood irresolute. She sat on the end of the bed. She would miss this room, which would not remember her or register any trace of her passage.

'So you're going back? To UK?'

'It's not back. This was back. I don't know.'

As the car drove through Bombay – behind VT, then up Tulsi Pipe Road and through Parel, she looked down from the flyovers to the small balconies and windows of chawls, decorated with plants in hanging pots, clothes drying, here and there a man in a vest.

Her mother, wearing sunglasses, talked about the servants at home, about a friend of hers who was unwell, about whether they'd be home in time for lunch. The sun grew higher and hotter. Leela thought of the hostel, of her room, and of the sea at Marine Drive, sparkling, impersonal.

She sent Sathya an email at his non-work address, asking if everything was all right, saying she'd heard about his mother's illness and that she was sorry. Another paragraph began:

You might have heard from Joan that I

She stared at it and pressed the backspace key.

A day later she sent a text: Hope you are okay, so sorry to hear about your mother. Let me know if I can do anything. Leela.

She called a day after that.

'Ah, Leela.' His voice sounded not only older but further away, as though transmitted by radio from the 1950s.

'How are you?' She was in her room, on the bed, half cross-legged. She stared with concentration at a cupboard.

'Not great. Amma died yesterday.' She was relieved he was so matter-of-fact.

'What happened?'

'She just – she hadn't been well for some time, we kept going for tests. Suddenly it turned out she had this thing. It started in the breast. Then it was everywhere –' But now he was weeping. It sounded like sniffing and swallowing. 'She was in a lot of pain at the end, that's the really fucking awful part. Sorry Leela.'

'Don't say sorry. I'm sorry,' Leela said.

'Everyone's sorry.'

'Shall I – do you want me to come for –?'

'It was this morning. Don't come now. Everyone's here – relatives, friends. People have been very nice, neighbours sending food and stuff. Come in a couple of weeks when it's quieter.'

'Okay. I'll call you in a few days to find out.'

'Leela, lots of people are turning up. Let me call you back in some time.'

He rang off. She went into the drawing room. 'Sathya's mother died.'

'Your friend from the office?' asked her mother.

'What happened?' asked her father.

Leela sat down at the table. 'Cancer. It was sudden. She wasn't well, then all of a sudden she was diagnosed. I didn't even know. Just yesterday. I just spoke to him. I'll go there, but not yet.'

The familiar things of her home – a red melamine bowl on a cupboard near the table, a brass vase that her mother had had the servant polish but which hadn't yet been used, a set of the pills her parents took with their breakfast – looked different, like a stage set. Sathya must be thinking that now, looking at the furniture of his mother's life and imagining clearing it away. It was a fact that a person was there at one time, and your ideas of her were so strong, the attachment and antipathy she inspired, and then she was gone in a final way. The ideas remained in you, what did you do with them? The clutter too. At fourteen, she had helped her mother clear out her grandparents' house: boxes of books, a trunk of letters, saris with rents in them, a hoarded box of Camay soap.

Many of those things had migrated to this apartment with her parents.

She eyed her father now. Mr Ghosh was reading. He looked up and caught his daughter's eye. 'Terrible,' he said, with genuine sympathy. His glance was again caught by the book.

31

How strange, she thought, lying under a tree in the park, the white military buildings of the Mall opposite, sun glancing in. She moved some hair to shade her eyes, and looked up through the leaves, maple-shaped, green, as though pasted on the blue enamel sky.

At home the rains had started and it was cooler in the daytime, sometimes sweater weather. Here, in London, she was wearing shorts and a t-shirt, lying on the grass and looking at the sky. Summer had appeared with the unreality it always had in northern Europe.

And I am here, she thought, her mind lazy, her eyes open to the blue, the leaves printed above, occasionally a flash of sun. A car would go by. I am here ... I was there. No, first I was here, a boy ran by, a little boy, with a small bicycle and his father following him, calling, 'Martin!'

I am here, I was here before, then I was there. Before that too, I was there.

There was a book beside her; her finger marked the place. A bottle of water, a small bag. The interview had seemed to go well. This weekend, she would see Neeti in Manchester. There was a train from Euston this afternoon.

The date, the 26th of June, stuck in her head, it meant something. She breathed the scent of grass, thought of another sunny day, the honey walls of a Cambridge college, white wine, poached salmon. The same date as their graduation. I must tell Amy. Her stomach twisted at the thought of

Vikram, his misery, and in a different way, Sathya and his. Again a picture of her and Amy, but seen from outside, as though figures in photographs, at the sunlit lunch. With what other eyes I used to watch – if I be he that watched … Not me, she thought of the memory. The me was slippery, it would not be found, the I, she waited for it. Another car passing, voices. There is a story that connects that place and that person with this one, with now. Somehow I got here. But I don't want to tell that story, and besides I don't remember all of it.

To be flat on the earth, it made you feel safe. The world might be turning but you would not at this time fall from it into space.

The train left from Euston. To get to Euston you – the blue line. But here – the brown line. She would work it out. Amazing not to remember, when you considered how much time the other self used to spend underground.

Heat infused the skin, the eyelids. She hadn't long to wait, simply some time to kill before the train. And, now, eternity. Eternity and a train to catch.

There was a story behind it. Who could recall?

However, the air smelled lovely: warm, flowery, of hay.

She lost herself. Something fell on her face, and she lifted it and sat up sleepily. A leaf, green, but a part of it yellowed.

Silence; then, not far away, a couple of men kicking a ball. Leela looked at the leaf, put it in the book to mark her place, and got up to walk towards the train.

Acknowledgements

Thank you: My parents, Vivan, Siddharth, Janani, Chinmayee, Katy, Eveliina, Veda, Kate, Nil, Jill; Amit Chaudhuri and Andrew Cowan for reading and commenting on the manuscript; Peter Straus and all at RCW; Mark Richards and all at Fourth Estate.

Special thanks to the home team: Sam and Lola B.